The Sound of Murder

Insurance agency programmer Dana Sanderson only wants peace and quiet at work. Then the investigation of a rash of suspicious natural death claims lands on Dana's laptop.

Failure means huge payouts for the company. Success means a huge bonus for her.

Will Dana's risks outweigh her reward?

GS-304

Mighty explorers of the galaxy Portarr and Flandarr inspect a non-descript watery planet in G-Sector.

A specimen that refuses to be a subject changes their lives.

Join the intrepid adventurers as they discover a strange beast that conquers their hearts.

Renovations

Bob Henderson despises the modern world.

Talking elevators. Automated cars. Smart phones that track every move, mood, and thought.

When his office building grows security cameras in the halls, Bob realizes the modern world might despise him right back.

The Garbage Belt

Looking for humans? Just look for the garbage.

Humanity takes a long time to learn how to manage limited resources, too. The rare and precious get lost with the useless and plentiful.

Meet Gayle Simmons, pilot of the Treasure Hunt.

Rare and precious, in her sights.

Sunlit Dispositions

A space station just exploded, and the Sunlit Spirit Empire calls in Alex, Free Troubleshooter extraordinaire. No last name needed.

Alex wades into the strange world of Sunlit Spirit intrigue, gamma blaster in hand.

Join Alex as he learns the deceptions behind the Truth.

Near Future Forward

Copyright © 2019 by Kari A. Kilgore and Jason A. Adams

All rights reserved

Published 2019 by Spiral Publishing, Ltd. www.spiralpublishing.net

Book and cover design copyright © 2019 by Spiral Publishing, Ltd.

Cover art copyright © 2019 by rolffimages | Depositphotos.com

ISBN-13: 978-1-948890-21-2

Large Print ISBN-13: 978-1-948890-26-7

LOC NUMBER: 2019911689

To Loston Wallace

An inspiration to creative folks everywhere.
And a good friend.

NEAR FUTURE FORWARD

FIVE SCIENCE FICTION SHORTS

KARI KILGORE

JASON A ADAMS

SPIRAL PUBLISHING, LTD.

CONTENTS

THE SOUND OF MURDER

KARI KILGORE

For Audrey

*Who has her own superpowers
and isn't afraid to share them.*

Chapter 1

THE INHABITANTS OF THE VAST, pale gray cubicle farm were more restless than usual on an early Friday afternoon. The endless rows of low fabric walls normally created a muffled silence long before five o'clock, neat desks abandoned as soon as possible for weekend freedom.

This week, though, end of quarter deadlines loomed over everyone's heads. The prospect of missing their bonus numbers tended to drive the insurance agents and adjusters more than a little bit insane.

Dana Sanderson guarded the calm routines of a programmer more fiercely than usual as muttering, pacing, and understated cursing swirled around her.

The new so-called team-building pods—otherwise known as introvert torture chambers—didn't bother with full-height walls. She had to make do with barely shoulder-height protection on three sides.

As a mid-level code cruncher, Dana knew it would be years before she'd have the simple pleasure of a door she could close. Even if she hunched behind her monitors, the sense of exposure never quite left her.

On the whole, the job was better than most she'd had over the last ten years. The building was in the middle of a typical soulless industrial park, but it was on the Commu-Share transit line. When Dana had to drive for some reason, she could plug in to free charging stations. The cafeteria was subsidized and surprisingly good. The huge selection of free holo-training, covering everything from programming languages to online security to financial planning was the best she'd ever seen. Best of all, outside of the four manic times of year, she could work from home at least one day a week.

If only her micro-managing boss would close his own door a little more often, Dana could probably get away with the great sin of listening to her own music. She sat close enough to his office that she would see the gate to his inner sanctuary opening in time to stash her contraband headphones.

Mr. Redmond would never tolerate such a lack of control, though, certainly not during crunch time when he prowled around like a big cat anxious for his feeding. A white noise machine placed carefully between her and the most fidgety of her co-workers helped. A little.

The soft, unobtrusive, and therefore maddening chime broke through Dana's concentration. She would have sworn her workstation had a sensor rigged to go off when she was really focused.

Sure enough, the incoming work request icon flashed red on her second monitor.

Before she could pull up the message, scratching noises against the metal cubicle frame behind her knotted up her already tense shoulders. She spoke without moving.

"Hi, Mr. Redmond."

"Ms. Sanderson. Just sent you a work order. Wanted to make sure you saw it."

Dana stretched her face into a silent scream, then shifted to polite curiosity before she turned around. Her manager wore his usual dark gray suit even on casual Friday, a walking sign of approval for the dreadfully bland office décor.

An odd scent competed with his normal expensive cologne of the month, soft floral notes clashing with assertive spicy musk. At the very least he livened up the stale, recycled office air when he circled by.

"Yes, sir. I have the work request right here."

Mr. Redmond nodded gravely. "It's marked urgent."

"I do see that, yes," Dana said, grasping on to her politeness.

"Let me know if you have any questions."

He walked away, jingling the change in his pockets, surely kept just for that irritating purpose. Not even Dana's grandparents had coins anymore.

"Yes, Mr. Redmond, I do have questions," she said under her breath. "Why do you think I can't check my own work reqs? Why do you scratch instead of knocking? And where do you even get that blasted change to jingle these days?"

She blew air out through her lips, then turned to see what was so vitally important.

Dana was shaking her head before she got through the first paragraph. No, this wasn't her department, not her job at all. Eleven cases, all young and healthy, death benefit claims under dispute. She was a programmer, not an insurance adjustor, no matter who paid her salary at the moment.

Her remarkably annoying manager had not only managed to send the job to the wrong person, he'd followed up before she could even open the silly thing.

She grabbed the mouse to bounce it right back to him, but a flashing note beside the Reject button caught her attention.

Investigation of underlying algorithms required before claims may be processed.

"Can't get out of this one so easily, Dana," she whispered as she picked up the phone. If she had to dig into code written before she was born, she wanted backup from someone who'd been with the company at least that long.

"Jackson here."

"Hey Gayle, Dana here. Listen, I just got a work req that doesn't make any sense. Did you work on the original algorithms for the risk rating tables? The ones for-"

"Yeah, your numbskull manager wouldn't get off my back about that. I'm the one suggested you. Need a fresh pair of eyes. Redmond's sure they don't work. I'm sure they do. Sorry, kid." And she was gone.

Dana snorted and hung up. Her grouchy old mentor was the one throwing her into this particular mess, not offering her a way out. Well, wrong department or not, she was stuck. She skimmed the notes again.

Six men, five women. Eleven marked at the lowest mortality risk, all dying far too young of natural causes over the past month. They lived in different parts of the country and didn't know each other. The only common thread was their life insurance company and their unusual deaths.

She drummed her fingers on the desk, vaguely aware she was contributing to the anxious noise in the office for a change. Dana clicked through to the individual files, but they didn't make any more sense. No evidence of any risky habits or hobbies in the investigation reports.

Only heartbroken families.

This kind of thing was exactly why she hated getting into this side of the business. The code and numbers might frustrate her, but they never depressed her.

She'd do her best, but she secretly hoped the claims held

up. Some of them were even younger than her twenty-seven years.

Three hours later, Dana stood and stretched, grimacing when her back and neck crackled. The code wasn't the problem here. Every line was as perfect as Gayle said.

Dana kept her smile to herself as she walked to Mr. Redmond's office, rehearsing under her breath.

Sorry, sir. We have to pay up, and expedite it for pain and suffering because we delayed in the first place.

The source of her manager's strange smell was clear to Dana's nose sooner than her eyes. The sweetish stink came from a new diffuser gadget sitting on Mr. Redmond's massive glass desk.

He had the overhead lights off, as usual, so only faint sunlight from outside competed with the spherical steam machine's blue glow.

No doubt yet another miracle cure he'd soon try to force onto all of them, just like yoga, meditation, and sunlight bulbs over the past several months. He never seemed to notice he was increasing everyone else's stress by pushing the next sure-fire solution he'd found while desperately trying to reduce his own.

"No, there's something going on here, some risk we're not seeing," Mr. Redmond said when she finished explaining what she'd found, leaning back in his high-backed brown leather chair. Dana wondered how many decent programmer's chairs the company could buy for what that high tech ergonomic miracle cost. "It may be a weird food trend or cure-all supplement they're taking now."

Dana forced herself not to add a snarky comment about the smell.

"I'm not sure what I can do about miracle cures, sir, long as they're legal. Everything I can see checks out."

"Well, you haven't checked everything. This is a huge

pool of claims, Ms. Sanderson. If these pay out, we'll have to recalculate all the damned tables and formulas. No one wants that. I have to be sure everything is on the level. I need you to dig into this, see what you can come up with."

"Beyond looking into the code, I'm not sure what I can do."

Mr. Redmond sat forward and folded his hands on his desk, staring into her eyes.

"I'm not supposed to bring things like this up, but I know about your past, Dana. You're the poster child for turning your life around after a rough start."

Dana stared at her own hands twisting in her lap, willing her face not to turn red. No one was supposed to know about her troubles as a kid, hacking into far too many phones and webcams and online accounts, learning the hard way that it wasn't a game after all. She struggled to keep her voice from shaking.

"If you know about me, you know why I can't get back into hacking, Mr. Redmond. That part of my life is over."

"I'm not asking you to get into their bank accounts. Just find the common thread. Take a look, a *careful* look, and see what you come up with. Don't worry about your usual projects for now. There's a full year's salary bonus for whoever works this out."

"A full…" Dana shook her head, quite certain she'd misunderstood. "You're offering me a year's pay? How could it be worth that?"

She didn't have to do the math. That much money would pay off her college debts and everything else she'd racked up putting her past firmly behind her. The prospect of returning to her hacker life, even temporarily, felt slightly less dreadful now.

"These were all in our lowest risk pool," he said, raising

his eyebrows. "Several of them had policies worth ten times your salary. Trust me. It's worth it."

"Is it worth paying for meals while I'm stuck here?" she said, not sure why she was still resisting. "I'm not about to do this on my own computer at home."

"I'll get IT to give you a secure link out, and a laptop to use at your place if you change your mind. Here or there, use your company expense account and feast away. As a matter of fact, we need to keep this one confidential as much as we can until we know what we're dealing with. It'd be best for everyone if you wouldn't mind working from home."

Dana got to her feet. The chance to work at home for as long as this took, away from the glaring lights, constant mutter of other people—and Redmond's maddening scratching—finally met her selling point. Even more than the money did.

"Okay. Have them set it up and give me the laptop. I'll start Monday."

Chapter 2

ONCE SHE GOT over her irritation at having to postpone her escape from the office while IT configured her home access, Dana was pleased and only a little horrified at how easily hacking came back to her. She was plainly delighted to work much faster after several years of hunting down bugs in code. By the middle of the day, though, she only knew enough to cause more uncertainty.

The first common thread was a frequent shopping card at Pure Delights, a natural foods chain far too expensive for her own blood. Most of Mr. Redmond's own miracle stress reducers that he insisted everyone in the office simply *must* try had come from the same place. Annoying, but hardly sinister.

She was still missing the essential clue. Time to dig deeper.

Something as simple as archived social media was the first real break she caught. Deleted accounts were far more accessible than most people realized, even after the account holder was eligible for life insurance claims.

Every one of the clients had posted about high levels of

stress and anxiety, and their struggles to deal with it were eerily like Mr. Redmond's. That wouldn't have been nearly enough to go on, but all of them mentioned the same meditation program. One they'd heard about on the proudly old-fashioned corkboards by the front door of every Pure Delights store just a few weeks before they died.

Internal Oasis.

Dana knew almost nothing about meditation, despite her manager's best efforts, but she was pretty sure it wasn't fatal.

Nothing on the main sales website seemed unusual, except the option for cloud-based customized recordings, specified to match the client's needs and brain waves. Far-fetched, maybe, but hardly impossible.

She clicked through to the demonstration recordings, then pulled her headphones out of her bottom desk drawer. Part of her wanted to dare Redmond to protest, but he stayed in his office for a change. A woman's voice, tranquil almost to the point of being comatose, spoke into her ears.

"Welcome to your personal sanctuary of peace, calm, and satisfaction. Internal Oasis works with your brain's unique operating system to create the most effective meditation you'll ever find. Let us help you change your life, for the better."

"Has to be subliminal," Dana said under her breath, searching for reviews and fine print about Internal Oasis. A deeply buried company legal filing indeed mentioned subliminal and hypnosis technology.

Part of her wondered if this was a pointless search, driven by her manager's promise of financial reward. It hadn't occurred to her until after she agreed that even though Mr. Redmond didn't say it out loud, he almost certainly meant the year's salary would come with working it out to the company's favor.

She'd found nothing but dead ends so far. She couldn't

abandon the single connection she'd unearthed, no matter how vague. A grumpy IT lackey delivering a sleek new black laptop bag, muttering at her to be careful with the damn thing, made up Dana's mind.

Only one person she knew could help with something as tricky as hidden recordings: a life-long friend who analyzed sound for a living.

Andre Telkin answered on the third ring.

"Hey Dana! How's it going?"

"I'm good, Andre. Need your help with a little project here. Definitely on the confidential side."

"Oh, intriguing. I'm all ears!"

Dana laughed. Only a guy deaf from birth would make that joke. Andre's advanced cochlear implant, a nearly invisible microphone that translated sound directly to his brain, was just what she was counting on.

"Meet me at my place in about thirty minutes. I'll bring the pizza and beer."

Chapter 3

After four years in what had to be the most boring complex in all of Metro Atlanta, Dana was gradually starting to feel at home. Nothing had changed about the never-ending rows of identical tan brick buildings, or the fleet of last year's trendy e-cars clogging the winding roads every morning and afternoon.

Between a steady income, feeling like an adult at last in her late twenties, and getting more comfortable in her own skin that she'd ever dreamed possible, Dana finally had a clear idea of who she was and how to create that in her own home.

The walls didn't shift from a reclusive teenager's dark primary colors to more girly pastel shades, but she did add coordinating rugs and matching towels in the kitchen and bathrooms. Actual framed photos and paintings replaced the college kid's beat up holo-posters that constantly changed. She'd even been contemplating getting a nicer shifting image display for a bit of variety.

Much as Dana wanted to keep the space as clean as it was

neat, she knew she'd have to hire someone to do the dusting and such as soon as she could afford it.

She paced in her tiny home office, watching Andre staring at the brand new laptop Mr. Redmond had surprised her with. Neither her desktop at the office or the clunky laptop she dragged with her for work-at-home days were half as fast as this screamer.

Andre looked just as modern, with yet another pleasing angular arrangement of his kinky black hair, this time featuring a streak of dark red on one side. A thin cable, transparent so she could see the minuscule twisted wires inside, lead from the laptop's headphone jack to the magnetic connector behind his left ear.

Her friend's rock solid confidence in himself as a Southern, African-American, deaf, gay man had given Dana a goal to aspire to for more than ten years now. He was the one person still in her life, outside of her family, who knew of her criminal past and how hard she'd worked to leave that behind. She suspected he admired her for all of it.

Andre sat back, disconnecting the cable from his implant.

"I don't hear much in these samples, Dana. Right under the overly soothing music a voice is telling you how the program will solve all your problems, but that's standard sales talk. Common as 'But wait, there's more.' I doubt you could get your hands on anything they've already sent out. Just sign up for the program and see what happens. You could damn sure use a little relaxation."

"A bunch of people ended up dead after their special program," she said, following him into the living room. "That's a little too much relaxation even for me."

Andre leaned back on Dana's dark brown sofa he'd helped her pick out, pulling the longer side of his hair back down.

The pea-sized implant matched his brown skin perfectly, but he always did his best to keep it covered.

"Don't get your panties in a bunch," he said. "I want to keep you around as long as the supply of free food and beer holds out." Andre ducked the pillow Dana threw without spilling a drop. "You go get it set up, and I'll listen to them. For one thing, they won't be matched to my brain waves. For another, my magic ear will most likely hear whatever they've got buried under the real thing since I caught the sales pitch. You wouldn't believe the frequency range with this newest model."

Dana tapped her short, dark purple fingernails against her bottle. Andre's plan wasn't any more underhanded than what Mr. Redmond had already asked her to do.

And several hours of searching on her own hadn't exactly turned up an abundance of leads.

"Deal. I'll make an appointment at their office in Midtown tomorrow. Looks like they send them out two or three times a week. You free in the evening for a while?"

"Not free, but reasonable to rent. I'll get you my dinner order by tomorrow afternoon."

Chapter 4

ON THE FOURTH set of Dana's personalized recordings, the first showing up the same day Internal Oasis' friendly technician mapped her brain waves for three long hours, they hit pay dirt.

Andre turned fast enough to knock a stack of books and papers off the increasingly cluttered desk in her home office.

"Take a little care with the belongings, Telkin!" When she leaned over to pick up the mess, he grabbed her arm.

"Yeah, sure, be glad to. Just as soon as you log into your bank account and transfer a few thousand dollars to a mystery charity."

"What?" Dana whispered. Heat churned in her stomach. "You did *not* just hear that."

"Yes ma'am, I certainly did." Andre fumbled for one of the notebooks on the floor. "I don't think… You probably shouldn't listen, but let me write this down." He dragged the progress bar in the audio file back, scribbled furiously, then handed the page to Dana.

"This was in the middle of the relaxation speech? 'Your deepest desire for your greatest good is to donate ten percent of your available funds to this worthy charity'? Come on, this is serious."

"You think I'd make that up?" he said, glaring. "I heard it clear as I hear you, right under the smarmy synthesizers. At least dig around in the charity account, D. See where it leads."

His challenging look did a lot more to convince Dana than his words. She closed her company-issued laptop less than ten minutes later.

"They've got it buried under about ten layers of dummy corporations in both directions, but that account goes back to Internal Oasis. This still isn't enough to link them to murder."

He shrugged. "Then we don't confront them yet. Not until we've got the evidence. Gonna have to cough up the cash."

"A tenth of my money?" Dana's voice was loud enough to startle herself. "In case you haven't noticed, I'm not exactly living in luxury here. This isn't the most ethical of corporations. They've probably already been in my bank accounts, so I can't send them fifty bucks and be done with it."

"Well, if this goes nowhere, I'll pay half. But you know as well as I do we're way past coincidence here. If they don't think you're playing along, we'll never know."

"I regret ever getting mixed up in this mess, huge bonus or not." Dana rubbed her eyes. "Move over. Let me log in to my accounts. What the hell, I'll just add it to my expense report."

Chapter 5

Two days later, after listening to her seventh personalized mediation, Andre opened another beer and handed a fresh one to Dana.

"Good news and bad news , Dana my dear. At least Ms. Relaxation isn't asking for cash this time."

"What's she asking for, then? The keys to my apartment?"

"Kind of. Just visit this website." He handed her another page covered with his scrawling handwriting. A cryptic web address, jumbled numbers and letters, was circled at the bottom. "You'll feel ever so much better once you provide your savings accounts, credit report data, government account passwords, and any other identifying information you can think of. All your troubles will be a thing of the past."

Dana swallowed half the beer, shaking her head.

"I thought old-school identity theft died out twenty years ago. Seems pretty low tech for neural mapping. Then again, I never suspected it. I never checked criminal reports from this bunch, not once I got past the investigations into their deaths. It might have been in front of us the whole time."

Records like this were probably sealed, especially with everyone dead, but she couldn't leave an end this loose dangling. Andre paced behind her while she searched, a lot like Mr. Redmond would have done. Dana was so caught up in the chase that she could ignore him.

"I'll be damned. Sit still for a minute and listen to me, Andre. We may be into something bigger than we thought. Turns out our meditation clients did file complaints. Financial fraud, petty theft, and yeah, identity theft. None of them were ever resolved."

Her head was spinning with the rapid connections. Hot excitement flooded up from her belly, just like in her bad old days.

"Internal Oasis has more than a million clients," she said. "Even if they only had people roped in through Pure Delights, which I doubt, the haul has to be massive."

Andre's eyes widened, and he got up to pace again.

"Time to turn this in and get you out of danger. Me too, of course. If they're trying to protect an income stream that big, they're not going to let a couple of amateurs mess it up."

Dana nodded, but she turned away so her friend couldn't see her face. She didn't want him to know the thrill of pursuit had her firmly in its grasp.

She didn't care nearly as much about the bonus Mr. Redmond promised as she did about figuring out what was going on. Finding out what she wasn't supposed to know. What someone had gone to an effort to keep her from finding.

"I'll go in and talk to Redmond tomorrow," she said. "I'm not about to give these jerks my information. Expense account or not, they have more than enough of my money as it is."

Chapter 6

DANA WALKED into a quiet and somber office the next morning, far more so than on an ordinary work day. No one was meeting anyone else's eyes, and several people looked like they'd been crying.

When she walked toward Mr. Redmond's closed door, the hair on the back of her neck stood up. Every instinct she had was shouting at her to get out of there.

Before she could turn around, Mrs. Austin, the Director of Human Resources, walked out of Redmond's office.

"Oh, there you are, Ms. Sanderson. I was going to call you later, but we can do this right now."

Mrs. Austin stepped back inside Mr. Redmond's office and held the door. Dana couldn't think of anything else to do but walk in. The older woman settled herself into that huge leather chair, her gray streaked bun barely touching the bottom of the headrest. She folded her hands under her ample bosom.

The globe diffuser, photographs, books, and everything else of Mr. Redmond's had disappeared.

"Where's Mr. Redmond?" Dana said before she could think of something else.

"Well, that's part of what I need to tell you. Mr. Redmond passed away this weekend. He died in his sleep, apparently of natural causes."

Dana's stomach seemed to fall through the floor. She'd never really liked the guy, but this was too much. Her youthful paranoia, re-born with so much snooping around looking for conspiracies, was on full alert.

Had she somehow put him in Internal Oasis' crosshairs?

"I don't understand," she said, swallowing nothing but air through a bone-dry throat. "He seemed fine last week."

"Yes, it's tragic. No one knows that these things happen unexpectedly better than people in our line of work."

The list of clients Mr. Redmond had asked her to investigate flashed through Dana's mind. They'd all supposedly died of natural causes, too.

"That's what we do, I guess," Dana finally said. "I'm sorry to hear that, Mrs. Austin."

"Yes, of course. That brings me to the next part of what I need to tell you, and it's actually the harder part. We've run an audit of the company expense reports for Mr. Redmond's department over the past few weeks. Normal procedure for a change in management, of course, but your account has shown some distressing irregularities. Combined with Mr. Redmond's notes about your…past, that naturally leaves me no other option."

Dana's heart pounded. "No, wait, I can explain that. The expenses, I mean. That was an investigation Mr. Redmond asked me to do. He authorized the food and everything else. Ms. Steffens should have records of the whole thing, she had to approve it."

"I'll certainly ask Ms. Steffens about it when she returns,"

Mrs. Austin said with a tight smile. "She's having to cut her overseas trip short because of all of this. But I'm afraid I'm going to have to ask for your keys and credentials, Ms. Sanderson. You know the strict policies about the expense accounts."

"You're firing me? Before you talk to Redmond's boss?" A beat later, Dana's frozen brain finally caught up to the scope of her situation. "My past isn't public record, Mrs. Austin."

"It is most unfortunate that your juvenile record was in Mr. Redmond's files, but I can't ignore it now that I know. You're not fired. Not yet. Officially this is leave with full pay, as you'll find in our policy. I'll make every effort to resolve the situation, but please understand this is a serious violation. Ordering food after hours here and many times from your apartment is hard to justify, certainly on top of being out of the office so frequently. There's only so much I can do."

Mrs. Austin stood and held out her hand. Dana stared at it for a few seconds, then she handed over her keycard and badge.

"Is it okay if I pack up my desk at least?"

"Under my supervision," Mrs. Austin said, nodding. "Certainly. Any company property must remain, of course."

Dana's mind raced as she walked toward her desk, feet never touching the floor, wondering if any record of her having the secure laptop had been filed outside of IT.

It wasn't like she could get into more trouble at this point, certainly not compared with what happened to former clients of Internal Oasis.

She packed up her few personal belongings, not much more than a couple of photos, her old programming textbooks, and the headphones Mr. Redmond would never tell her not to wear again. She pulled her clunky company laptop out of the drawer, wondering how long before Mrs. Austin realized she hadn't bothered taking it home for weeks. She left it on the desk before she walked away.

Andre was right. This was a bigger mess than any of them imagined.

Chapter 7

Dana and Andre walked the exercise track around her apartment complex early that evening, the best way she could think of to soothe her newly born worry about her apartment being bugged.

Every step along the flawlessly manicured gravel track reminded her they were going in circles, avoiding the horror of the investigation only a dead man knew about.

Running a background snoop on Mr. Redmond had seemed like a good idea an hour ago, even with the risk of using her personal computer instead of the company one she didn't quite trust.

Finding his name on a list of recent new stockholders for Internal Oasis only made her fear and paranoia a thousand times worse.

"What do you mean, keep going?" Andre said, his voice sharp. "Your boss is dead, Dana. Another client of Internal Oasis going six feet under, and a stockholder to boot. You can't keep taking chances like this, and you definitely can't hand over your identity to a bunch of murderers."

Andre had a point, but her need to find the truth was

having none of it. She didn't even care about the money anymore.

"Listen to me," she said for at least the fifth time. "I'm not going to give them my information. I'm going to file a report on the transfers out of my bank account. Then if there's something going on, we can report them before there are more dead bodies out there."

Andre stopped, his fists clenched at his sides.

"What if they decide to take hands-on action this time? They might just skip the niceties and send someone over to cut both our throats!"

Dana put a hand on his shoulder, dismayed at how tense he was.

"No, that's not how they do this. Every single person I've dug up has died of what looks like natural causes. No violence, no drugs, no poison that anyone can find. We'll never know unless we do this, and they'll just keep getting away with it. Don't back out on me now, Dre."

He rolled his eyes at the much-hated nickname, but Andre kept walking.

"Fine, but you owe me. They shut down the expense account?"

"First thing this morning. That's what's about to get me fired, remember?"

"Then I'll spring for dinner tonight, you bum. But once you get your severance pay, you're taking me out on the town."

Nearly an hour after she filed the fraud report to her bank, Dana held her breath waiting for the apparently still secret company laptop to get online. The secure connection took a while every time, but she expected sirens and armed guards at any second.

"Wow, I'm surprised that worked," she said, letting out her breath. "HR must not know I have it."

"About time we caught some *good* luck. How long do you think it'll take for Internal Oasis to notice the report to the bank?"

"Good question. They caught my deposits fast enough, or at least they sent out the next recordings right away. What are you buying me for dinner? We've been through every delivery-"

"Hang on," Andre said, leaning toward the monitor. "I'm afraid your stomach's going to have to wait. Your new recording has arrived."

Dana's body ran hot, then cold. For the first time since this crazy trip started with that odd work order, she felt more than doubtful. Dana was terrified.

She'd probably already lost her job, and at least one more person was dead. Maybe this had gone on long enough.

"We're in over our heads, Andre."

"You noticed. Tell me something I don't know, D."

Their eyes met, and both fell into a mad fit of giggling. Most unbecoming and inappropriate for the situation, and the only possible way to go through with it.

"I guess we can't stop now. Plug in and see what she has to say. If you start to fall asleep on me, I'll knock you silly."

"Too late," Andre said, grinning. "But stand by just in case."

As he'd done since the strange messages started, Andre scribbled the words as he heard them, talking to himself under his breath. This time, Dana sat beside him and watched, tapping her foot.

After almost fifteen minutes, he gasped and turned to her. His face was as close to pale as she'd ever seen it.

"What? What did Ms. Relaxation say?"

"Ms. Relaxation said die." He ran a hand over his face, then took a deep breath. "She counted down again, like she does at the beginning. Relax, feel heavy, drop down into your quiet self, heart rate slowing, the whole works. But after one, under that damn warbling keyboard music, she said your heart will slow to stillness. Your troubles are at an end."

"Are you sure?"

Even after everything else she'd found, everything they'd found together, Dana wasn't ready to believe this.

"Positive."

"You think that would really work? Telling someone's heart to just stop like that?"

Andre shrugged, but his jaw worked like he was trying not to throw up.

"Think about it, Dana. They've already worked out how to get their clients to give up their money, their security, their whole identities. People go to subliminal clinics all the time for weight loss, smoking, drinking, whatever they want a quick fix for. It's not like the bad old days, either. This stuff works. Internal Oasis hasn't exactly been demonstrating the best corporate ethics, have they?"

Dana hugged Andre hard, surprising a grunt out of him.

"You did it, Andre. You figured it out."

"Oh, come on," he said, rolling his eyes. "That's bull, and you know it. I expect my share of any reward money, mind you, or at least a great party, but this was your ballgame. You found the pattern. You kept going when it didn't make sense to anyone else. All I did was lend you my bionic ear."

"I have to hear it."

He swatted her shaking hand when she reached for the speaker to disconnect the cord to his implant.

"No *way*, Dana. Didn't you hear a word I just said? I'll get this analyzed and broken down into the separate tracks tonight, but you know you can't listen to it. There's no coincidence here, not a chance. The day you filed the fraud report, this showed up? I'm willing to bet my savings account and yours too that all the rest of them heard the same thing as soon as they stirred up trouble. Personalized and tuned to their exact brainwaves."

"Gods, we did lead them right to Mr. Redmond," Dana said. She swallowed several times, trying to keep her stomach moving in the right direction.

"He probably did that himself. He put you on the case, remember? Invested in them a month ago, then started poking around in those death claims with no idea where it would end up. I bet we'd find some suspicious transfers out of his bank account if we looked. They didn't go after you until you filed the bank fraud complaint."

"We're talking about murder here, Andre. Murder by meditation."

As soon as the words were out, Dana was again fighting the urge to laugh. She clenched her fists until her hands ached to stop it. This went beyond their normal level of tasteless jokes. Andre only nodded, his features grave.

"You got it. Now we have to make sure everyone knows about it."

Chapter 8

DANA'S DAYDREAMS of great public outcry and uproar never made it past the *what if* stage.

Andre wouldn't tell her where he sent all of the recordings and notes, but less than a week later Internal Oasis quietly went out of business. The industry newsfeeds went silent after a few startled reports.

She'd already hacked into a forum for everyone who'd lost their jobs by the time the founder and CEO, a voiceover actress named Teresa Jeanette, ended up in prison. Nothing there or in the news mentioned the remarkable brain mapping technology.

Dana wondered if that was already in the hands of the government. Or worse.

Former employee gossip ran toward tax evasion as the cause of the whole thing. No one doubted whatever happened had been hushed up, and fast. Probably at great expense.

Dana and Andre kept the truth to themselves.

The only person Dana didn't leave in the dark was Mrs. Austin. She'd visited her old office the same day Andre turned everything in. She didn't tell her friend she was going, though she did give him credit for the vital part he played.

Sitting in front of the woman who'd fired her, trying not to fidget, sweating, and forcing herself to keep talking when the HR manager clearly didn't believe a word of it was hard enough. Facing Andre when it all came to nothing would be intolerable.

After that horrifying meeting, Dana occupied herself with the long search for another job.

Her first call came from her old one.

"Ms. Sanderson? Bonnie Austin here. I have good news for you."

"About the Internal Oasis investigation?"

"Among other things. I'm also calling to offer you your job back."

Dana had to try several times before her voice functioned.

"You want…" Dana shook her head, trying to force her brain to catch up. "You're asking me to come back?"

"Everyone in management hopes you will, yes." Mrs. Austin paused, then went on in a strained voice. "I do too, of course. Your work exposing the criminal activities of Internal Oasis was outstanding. You're welcome to return to programming, but with your success in a difficult case, we're hoping you'll consider a transfer into our own investigation department."

"Wait, give me a minute to catch up," Dana said. She wished Andre were there to see her grinning like a madwoman. "What happened with those claims? The ones Mr. Redmond asked me to look into?"

"That's part of the good news. Those were all paid in full by Internal Oasis, along with a healthy increase for wrongful death. I'm told many other deaths were linked to them with the same result, including Mr. Redmond's. You saved many more lives, and fortunes, by stopping them."

"I really wish Mr. Redmond were here to see this," Dana said, surprised by a tear rolling down her cheek.

"We all do. He was instrumental in getting the right woman for the job involved by recruiting you. In fact, that brings me to the third bit of good news. Your report to me allowed a further investigation into Mr. Redmond's confidential activities leading up to his tragic demise. Between that and talking to his manager, we were able to verify everything, including the bonus he promised you. You've certainly earned it. The full amount will be deposited by the end of the month. We'd like to offer an equal reward to your friend as well."

"I don't know what to say, Mrs. Austin." Dana was fighting giggles that felt uncontrollable now, and in danger of losing that fight. "I, uh, thank you!"

"Thank you for all your hard work, especially for continuing after our unfortunate misunderstanding. The truth might never have come out otherwise. Take a few days to think it over. I hope to hear from you soon."

Dana ended the call, her hands shaking so badly she had to try three times. She would have given a chunk of the money, perhaps ten percent, to see Mrs. Austin's face when she offered the programmer with a criminal past not only her job back, but a promotion where she'd be paid to *use* that past. Not sneaking around off the record, either, but right out in the open.

No small, ordinary celebration would do for such a bizarre turn of events, and Dana could only think of one person up to the task.

Their long shared history of themed birthday parties, often including sweet, silly costumes complete with tiaras and glitter, provided the perfect inspiration. She managed to connect the call on the first try.

"Andre! Get yourself and your magic ear over here, now! You're about to star in that grownup superhero party of our daydreams!"

GS-304
JASON A. ADAMS

For Gosamer, who was indeed a good boy.

Chapter 1

Portarr, commander of the bioship Keelaa, took nour-
ishment while he waited on his young assistant to complete
the study preparations. The savor of this small watery planet's
life forms was different, as could only be expected, but quite
tasty. He quickly slurped the last of the tiny viviparite's
entrails as Flandarr signaled all was ready.

Portarr stared at the new specimen as Flandarr processed
the intake. Around him, the fibrous walls of the ship were
just beginning to bud with new growth. Something to do
with the yellow light of this mediocre star on the outer
galactic rim certainly agreed with the Koeden physique.
Certainly Portarr was feeling as spry as the bioship. The craft
still hummed with pleasure in the warm golden glow, and
Portarr hummed as well. The scent of fresh biomass was
wonderful after so many dark and dead units spent in
quantum drive.

He and Flandarr, like generations of Koeden before
them, were travelers and scientists. They wandered from
system to system, cataloging and studying the life forms they
encountered, or marking uninhabited worlds based on their

potential for later resource extraction. Thus did the youth of his kind burn off excess foolishness and energies, while providing useful knowledge to their homeworld-bound elders. He envied the bioships, which made thousands of journeys over dozens of Koeden lifespans. He himself had few journeys remaining.

On this trip, they had selected an obscure world in G-Sector of the Rotgarr quadrant. The planet had an abundance of water and rich growing medium, of which a bewildering variety of un-manipulated vegetation took full advantage. So much so that the atmosphere would have been quite toxic with oxygen for the Koeden, were it not for an equal variety of animal life, which filtered the poisonous gas into carbon dioxide. A symbiotic relationship which Portarr had encountered before, but never to such a balanced level.

He stepped through the portal, the rigid vine curtain parting as the room recognized his pheromones, and stood beside his shorter companion. Flandarr was nearly chartreuse in his excitement, relishing his first journey as Prime Xenologist. He was yet a youngling, still nearly spheroid and only slightly larger than their subject. A good showing here, with proper deportment on his next two or three travels, and he would replace Portarr as Keelaa's commander.

None too soon, he thought. Portarr towered over the Xenologist, his own body more cylindrical and rigid with age. A secondary tentacle rose to scratch the emerging bud vesicles on his torso, now indigo with the coming change. Soon he would be forced to leave voyaging behind as his body morphed into first seeding, then budding offspring. He would choose a new name, and Tamrii would no longer be his reproductive mate, but instead his teacher and mentor. He would miss the traveling, but once rooted that would be impossible. Still, no time for such maudlin meanderings now.

The Commander noted the careful way his protégé had painstakingly reproduced the creature's observed habitat. Convincing the ship to grow such odd quarters had taken a bit of doing, and Portarr doubted he could have managed half so well himself.

The quarters were squared off as much as the ship would tolerate. The floor now resembled the fur of the planet's more shaggily-haired vertebrates. The ship managed to produce a bioluminescent sphere hanging from several filaments to light the space, and a large sleeping platform with a firm yet spongy surface stood against the wall to complete the room. Everything was naturally shaded in brown, green, and vermillion, but from what they had seen, color coordination was not overly important on this planet. Of necessity and need for further study some of the incidentals were missing, but Portarr was sure Flandarr would be able to coax those out of their sometimes recalcitrant ship, given time.

"Tell me of this creature, Flandarr," he said. The specimen, a medium-sized example of what appeared to be the elite life form of this planet, lay on the sleeping platform. The soporific had yet to wear off, but nothing in the specimen's scent or bioscans seemed to indicate a dangerous reaction.

"I have labeled it GS-304, Commander" said Flandarr. "I rescued it from a caregiver biped that was attempting to apprehend it, to put it in a cage on a transport. I think the biped might have seen me, but he was distracted by a small electronic communications device and I was able to spray them both with soporific before it could react."

"And the biped? Where is it now?"

"I left it behind. You said we should only retrieve one of the higher creatures, after all." Flandarr appeared calm enough, but a faint orange pulsing revealed his worry.

"Quite right, Prime," Portarr said. "I believe we learned

enough by observation to adequately replace the bipeds' care-giving functions." They both chuckled. The bipeds seemed fairly simple, so emulation would cause no difficulty.

The creature was stirring slightly, and Flandarr signaled the ship to reduce lighting to an approximation of dawn in the specimen's local zone. Its jaws gaped widely as it raised its head.

All at once, GS-304 was on its feet, all four of them, head cocked forward, and emitting a low rumble. The copper-colored hairs along its dorsal ridge rose as its body stiffened. Its eyes flicked between the two Koeden.

Portarr was surprised at how menacing the whole image was. Flandarr had green lines of fright pulsing and twining across his torso.

The specimen turned slowly in a complete circle, never stopping the rumble. When it came back around to them, the noise suddenly stopped. GS-304 sat on its haunches and hung its head. Now it sounded a soft, cyclic keening note.

"I believe GS-304 realizes it's a captive," Flandarr said.

"Astute observation, Prime," Portarr said, one primary tentacle caressing the younger officer's head while his secondary pair coiled a bit in amusement. Then seeing his companion's color shifting toward embarrassment, he relented.

"We cannot be sure yet what its vocalizations signify, can we? Are these sounds its primary form of communication? Give me your best hypothesis."

Flandarr was somewhat rigid, but replied promptly enough. "Best guess is that the sounds are too simple to be language by themselves. I believe the main form of commu-nication is a combination of pheromonal scent and physical display. Note the position of its body and head, which even *we* can recognize as submissive."

Flandarr had extended a tentacle as he spoke. Both he

and Portarr flinched as the creature raised its head and extended its proboscis to lick the tip of one manipulator digit, but it didn't seem dangerous.

The Xenologist recovered quickly. "Look, Commander," he said. "I believe GS-304 wants to establish relations."

"Quite so, Prime. But it might also be testing your palatability."

Flandarr jerked back, but extended his digits again when the specimen gazed at him, its rearmost appendage waving slowly back and forth. He touched one of its aural receivers, rubbed lightly, and the creature leaned against him. Clearly it enjoyed the contact.

"I saw a caregiver doing this with another one," Flandarr said, his own aural fibers coloring slightly. "It appears to be a common activity, possibly a bonding ritual."

"Excellent," Portarr said, stroking the youngling reassuringly. Interesting that their two species understood the same touch response. "What else did you observe that might help you with the subject?"

Flandarr went into a recital of the various activities he'd seen the GS creatures and their caregivers engaged in. Some were obvious, such as feeding and grooming. Others were more esoteric. For instance, the GS species was very hygienic and giving, eliminating waste products where a wide variety of vegetal life could benefit. Yet for some reason, they let their caregivers eliminate inside the dwellings. He shuddered, but remained a scientist. Perhaps the odd collection vessels and tubing swept the material away to be stored or composted.

Portarr let his Prime rattle on, not really listening. His aural fibers would record everything and he'd listen more intently later. Right now, he was fascinated by the biology of the specimen. It weighed 23.6 kraden in their gravity, which was very close to that of the planet below at sea level. Heavy for its size. That was the protein-based flesh and calceous internal framework, of course. It was also the fluid content, far higher than that of himself and the other Koeden.

His kind was also carbon-based, but more akin to the apparently insentient vegetation of GS-304's home. Only the animals of this world seemed capable of motion and thought. Peculiar that what amounted to fragile fluid sacks had thrived, but not terribly uncommon in the galaxy. Whatever frameworks for intelligent life were possible had probably evolved on some planet or other. Such was his belief, and the belief of most of his caste.

Portarr finally waved across Flandarr's vision, cutting off the lecture.

"Enough, young Prime," he said. "I have full confidence that you are well equipped by your natural talents and keen synopsis of GS-304's habits and those of its minions to carry on with the project."

"Thank you, Commander," Flandarr said, glowing with pride. "I shall continue to study the specimen, and attempt to gain its trust. I hope to have a full report ready in four or five of this planet's rotations."

Chapter 2

Portarr awoke from dormancy several hours later. He took a few moments to shift and bend as much as possible, trying to offset the lignin buildup which was becoming more of a handicap as his body marched inexorably toward the rootfield of age.

As he moved out to the pantry area, hoping to find a few more of the lovely rodents he'd sampled the day before, he felt cilia and root hairs snapping back into his lower extremities as he raised his limbs into his working footwear. Already his cursed body was trying to tie him to the ground.

No, that was uncharitable. He'd had his time gallivanting around the cosmos, and now he would have to take his turn budding the next generation. He hoped they would all be happy that he'd lost the joys they would find.

He entered the laboratory, his greeting to Flandarr dying away as he looked across the empty observation area, into the empty specimen room. Where was his Xenologist? Where was the creature?

Portarr moved as quickly as he could back to the main control area.

He could not stop the horrible visions that came to him; visions of white bony teeth tearing through vulnerable pith.

Flandarr was not old enough to have much lignin. He was yet soft, and would be easy prey to the foul beast's rage.

He stepped into the hanging mossy growth of the bioship's direct interface. He formed the explanation of what had happened in his mind's eye, trying to express all his worry for his friend, and his anger at what that protein monster had—

The ship blocked the images from his mind, replacing them with a visual from Flandarr's dormancy chamber. Portarr gaped, trying to understand what he was seeing.

On a raised platform similar to the one in the specimen's chamber, only concave to match Flandarr's form, the Xenologist lay prone. GS-304 lay against him, its body curving around his, also dormant.

Had they fought each other and both died? No, that made no sense. If that were the case, why the platform? He sent a query to the ship, which made no reply except a feeling of amusement.

Portarr took a quark streamer from the weapons locker, checked the charge was full, and rushed to Flandarr's chamber. He stood beside the platform, unsure how to proceed. Finally, he simply poked his Prime on a sensory orb.

Flandarr jerked, and his movement woke the specimen. The Xenologist rolled upright, causing GS-304 to flop into the vacated hollow. It floundered to its feet, looked sleepily up at the Commander, and spread its horrifyingly huge maw, showing all its many pointed and serrated teeth.

It would kill both of them. Chew them both to nothing more than a pile of fibers.

He covered the creature with the weapon. "Steady, Flandarr. Do not fear. Move slowly away from the creature and I'll—"

Flandarr finally focused on Portarr, then on the beam thrower in his grasp.

"Commander!" he said. "What are you doing? Do not shoot! Gosamarr is my guest!"

Portarr slowly lowered the streamer, feeling more shock than his stiffening visage could display.

"Your *guest*?" he said. "What do you mean, your guest? Why is it not in its chamber?" He looked down at the specimen, then back toward Flandarr. "*Gosamarr*? What is this?"

"Well," the Prime began, an array of conflicting coloration rippling across his body, "GS-304 seemed terribly objectifying, especially as I am working to create a bond of trust and mutual respect. I have still not been able to understand more of its communications than the basics, so I do not know what Gosamarr calls itself, so I made something up. I like it, and he seems to as well, don't you Gosamarr?"

Flandarr was stroking the floppy aural appendages again. The thing's fleshy mouthparts rippled, and it closed its eyes and groaned.

Portarr counted slowly in his head. Eight…nine…ten….

"Why," he said, remembering the Prime's youth and his own respect for patience, "is it in *here,* instead of in the laboratory where it belongs?"

"He was alone and frightened," Flandarr said, still rubbing Gosamarr. "I have seen many of his kind reposing with their caretakers. Both species appear to take comfort in the arrangement, so I thought he might appreciate it if I provided a similar opportunity."

Sixteen…seventeen…

"And how do you know how it was feeling?"

"Keelaa told me. The ship is quite appreciative of Gosamarr's deposits and wished to repay his kindness."

"Fine," Portarr said, certain he'd not been so foolish when

he was a budling. "Only take it back to the laboratory now. I do not wish it to be a disruption."

"I must ask you to reconsider, Commander," Flandarr said. "I feel we can learn more from Gosamarr if we interact in a more open manner. Let us befriend the subject, rather than merely study him."

"*It*, you mean," Portarr said. "We have no way of determining gender."

"I have indeed determined gender," Flandarr said, perking up again. "I have been able to intercept some of the planet's training materials for the caregivers. Let me show you."

Flandarr tickled two interface webs from the nearest wall, and wrapped one around each of their heads. Images burst into Portarr's mind; bipeds of every sort wrapped around each other in twos, threes, sometimes entire groups. Their artificial coverings were missing in most of these images, and in most the hairier ones were penetrating the smoother ones with what appeared to be ovipositors.

"Like many of the animal forms, the larger ones must be the females, which deposit the ova in the males for fertilization and germination," Flandarr said. "Obviously this requires a great deal of training, given the number and variety of educational images available."

"I am not certain you are correct," Portarr said, stepping out from the interface. "Yet you are the Xenologist. Continue your study, and we shall see. But first, take the specimen back to its chamber and perform your daily maintenance tasks."

"May I keep Gosamarr with me during my duty cycle, Commander?" Flandarr said. "Perhaps I will be able to teach him about us, and we may be able to learn a bit more of each other's language by working together on common goals."

Twenty-three...twenty-four...twenty-five...

"Fine," Portarr said, relenting to the youngling's eager plea. He pointed down at the creature, then tried the caress Flandarr had demonstrated. Yes, he did find it pleasant, and the creature seemed to as well. "You may keep it with you, but only if you do not let it disrupt anything."

Chapter 3

"Flaaaandaaarrrr!!!" Portarr bellowed. He was finished with counting.

He moved through the ship, looking for that imbecile of a Xenologist and the disposal unit he called Gosamarr.

Portarr found them in one of the storage areas. Flandarr hurled a small red sphere, which bounced off the walls only to be caught in mid-air by the graceful form of GS-304, who vocalized in sharp, staccato bursts as he waited for the next throw.

Portarr stopped in the entrance and watched, impressed by its athleticism. Very flexible indeed, especially—

He shook himself, remembering to be angry. One secondary tentacle flashed out and snatched the ball from the air, right in front of the specimen's air intake.

GS-304 yelped and nearly flipped backward. Both it and the Prime turned to see Portarr standing there. Flandarr pulsed a guilty green. The creature merely looked annoyed at being interrupted.

"Commander. How are you this fine—"

"Prime Xenologist, as your commander, I *order* you to take the specimen GS-304 and put it off the ship."

"Off the ship?" Flandarr said, confused. "But Commander, we are in orbit, approximately one hundred fifteen pridan above—"

"I do not care," Portarr said, pointing at the furry monster. "That…that *thing* has destroyed my footwear. My most comfortable set. Do you know how difficult it is to find tolerable footwear? At my stage? I shall not be able to enjoy any footwear much longer in any case, and now my favorites are nothing but scraps!"

"I am dreadfully sorry, Commander," Flandarr said, tentacle swaying placatingly. "I am sure Gosamarr merely wished to study them."

The Xenologist kept his body between that of his charge and Portarr.

"Study them? *Study them?*" Portarr's entire torso flashed violet with rage. "Do you often *study* things by partially digesting and then regurgitating them? On another's sleeping platform?" He whipped his tentacles around Flandarr, trying to grab the creature. The Prime's damned youthful spherism was too broad for his reach.

"Please, Commander!" Flandarr had backed against an alcove, Gosamarr safe behind his bulk. "Calm yourself! I will work with the ship on replacements. It is only footwear, and I'm sure Gosamarr meant no harm."

"It has also chewed on the ship's structures—"

"And Keelaa has been able to grow everything back. The ship finds it cute."

"There is hair everywhere. It keeps getting in my—"

"Keelaa and I have been cleaning twice a day to keep the hair issue under control. Gosamarr cannot help it, his hairs break off in the heat. It's our fault for not giving him cooler quarters."

Nine hundred forty seven…nine hundred forty eight…

"We are leaving," Portarr finally said. "In two units. I want GS-304 off this ship before it turns you into any more of a pet than you already are."

Flandarr turned the yellow of deep fear. "No, Commander! I beg you!"

"I said *off*!"

Flandarr muttered something.

"What was that, Prime Xenologist? I didn't quite hear you."

"I said I wish to keep him, Commander," Flandarr said, magenta with defiance. "I have more I can learn from him, and he trusts me. I do not wish to betray that trust."

"Flandarr, what did I say? I thought I said 'off,' or am I mistaken?"

"Please, Commander. At least let me return him to the surface safely. Keelaa can generate a landing pod."

"If you must," Portarr said with a sigh, trying to not be too much the elder-in-the-dirt. "But two units, and not one flicker more." He lumbered around with as much dignity as he could muster and tromped back toward the command center.

Chapter 4

Exactly 1.8 units later, Portarr watched through an external viewer as a large, woody pod shot forth into the planet's upper atmosphere, glowing brighter and brighter as it descended down to the upper clouds, then out of sight around the horizon.

Good riddance.

He heard Flandarr approach behind him, and spoke without turning.

"I am sorry I was so harsh, young Flandarr," he said as he stroked the bioship into acceleration mode, heading back toward the system's edge and the drop into Q-space. "I hope you had enough time to study the specimen—"

"Gosamarr," the youngling said.

"Yes, Gosamarr. I trust you can see now how it was training you to be a caregiver. I had to eject it for *your* sake, my good Prime. Your welfare is my responsibility."

"I understand," Flandarr said. "And I appreciate your concern, Commander. If you have no further need for me, I shall return to my quarters until we drop."

"Very well, Prime. Rest well."

Portarr watched him go, troubled by the lack of grief. The youngling had been so upset when told he had to dispose of GS-304. Now he was merely sullen. And was that a hint of green he saw? The ship was also acting peculiar.

Had he done wrong? He knew he'd made the best decision, but part of him felt a little sorry for Flandarr, and even for GS-304. They did seem to enjoy each other's company. Maybe his youthful companion received something from the furry alien that Portarr himself could not provide.

He might as well admit it, even if only to himself. He missed Gosamarr too. A *little*. He thought he could almost hear its rapid-fire signal from the levels below.

Ah, well. Perhaps he was growing paranoid. He would have a Med check his chemistry when they returned to the outpost.

He went back to the viewer and watched the blue planet dwindling swiftly behind them.

Across his vision, a lone coppery filament floated gently in a breeze from the ventilator.

Around him, the ship hummed with quiet satisfaction.

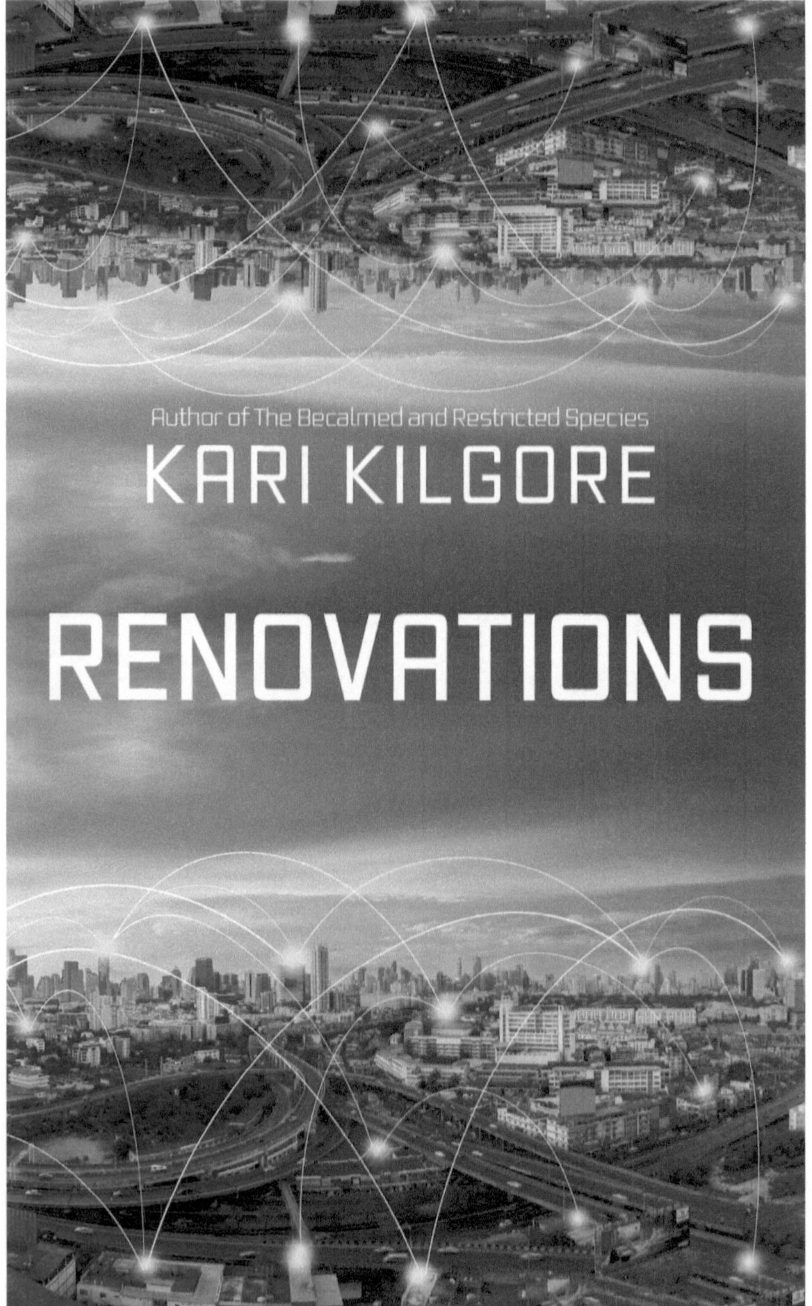

Author of The Becalmed and Restricted Species
KARI KILGORE
RENOVATIONS

For my mother-in-law Karen Adams

Who embraced new technology,
especially for her studies of the past.
And who always maintained a healthy respect
for the tools she used.

Chapter 1

THE EYES in the hall stopped Bob Henderson's heart.

Nothing else in the endless expanse of corporate offices had changed. Same polite beige walls hung with officially approved, bland artwork. Same muddy brown carpet with an inoffensive swirling pattern. And all the same co-workers scurrying about, striving to do just enough to fit in without standing out.

In the sixteen years Bob had been doing his level best to scurry while appearing to stroll, not so much as a single landscape or wildlife painting had changed. Not without a survey, results study, and staff meeting first.

Yet at the intersection of every smaller hallway and open space, a silvery, globe-like eye sprouted from the ceiling. Bob's arm hair tried to rise under his sleeves, made impossible by the black wool suit jacket he still had on from the latest corporate mucky muck meeting.

He forced air into his lungs, cringing away from his own sweat breaking through his heavy layers of deodorant and aftershave. He was certain he heard tiny cameras over the general office background noise, moving and focusing inside their concealing mirrored domes, recording every movement and sound.

No one noticed Bob frozen half out of the elevator. He didn't notice himself until his heart lurched back into action with a painful jolt. By the time the elevator politely asked if he needed help, his work partner Tim was several paces down the hall.

The system's voice sent Bob out like a shot.

Tim finally turned, forehead furrowed under his tidy blond corporate haircut.

"Bob, what's wrong?"

"It's not enough they have the computer controlling everything." Bob hoped he kept his now thundering heart and laboring lungs to himself. "That blasted Central Building Unit. Lights, phones, the whole damned building. Now they have to put cameras in the halls? Who told the CBU to do this?"

Tim stared at the row of gleaming half globes.

"I'm sure they're not cameras," Tim said. "They look like mirrors. Remember a few weeks ago when Cheryl ran into Walt coming around the corner too fast? They just programmed mirrors for safety."

"Without half a dozen survey emails?" Bob said, shaking his head. "If you believe that…"

Tim half-smiled in his folksy way that didn't calm Bob for a second.

"Hey, you and Carol coming by tomorrow night?" Tim said. "Steve says it should be a heck of a game, good as last time."

"Yeah, about that." Bob hated the way his face turned red, but that didn't change a thing. "Carol's not really around anymore." They both stopped outside Tim's office, and Bob knew word for word what Tim was going to say.

"You got into a another fight about the networks, didn't you?"

"Just like always, buddy. Knew I could count on you to help make a bad thing worse."

Tim stared at him for a second, not making a pretend nice face this time. Bob walked away before Tim could dispense words of wisdom. Somehow the one who'd been happily married since he was twenty-two years old felt qualified to give relationship advice to a forty-one year old newly single guy.

Bob counted three more of the mirrored globes along the hallway to his office. There was even one outside his door, hanging above his assistant's desk. Laura herself was nowhere to be found, but no need to worry about that. The blasted CBU would be able to find her in a second with these brand new eyes it was growing.

Even with his irritation at Tim and his unease about whatever now decorated the hall, Bob couldn't stop the excitement creeping around his grouchy edges. For the first time in months, nearly a year, one of his and Tim's projects had received full funding. Tim got on his last nerve sometimes, but this time his insistence on doing too much preliminary research had paid off.

Bob just wanted to savor this for a while.

He gritted his teeth at the number of new emails that popped up as soon as he activated the sleek, black touchscreen monitor. That could only be routine messages from the CBU for the two days he'd been gone for the funding meeting. Almost all of Bob's co-workers knew sending him email was a guaranteed waste of time.

Bob's gut soured from satisfaction to full-blown disgust as he read the most recent message. He'd just walked in the door, and already their project funding was cut in half and marked as preliminary. Unless he and Tim presented further findings, the whole thing would be scrapped. Findings he'd have to do himself, since do-gooder Tim had over-prepared as usual.

And of course, they had to present first thing tomorrow morning.

He couldn't possibly pull so much data together and manage to get out of the office before midnight. His righteous bout of pre-work seething was interrupted by a knock on his door.

Maybe he would leave at a reasonable hour after all.

"Bad news, Laura," Bob said before his assistant could speak. "New reqs for that big project. We've got another presentation in the morning."

"What do you need me do, Bob?" Laura sighed as she leaned against the doorjamb. "I've got to head out before seven."

"I doubt either of us will be leaving before ten."

He followed her out, deciding his ego could use a boost after such a rotten couple of weeks since Carol left. He stood behind Laura's chair as he told her the resources he needed. Close enough so her light brown hair moved with his breath, stirring up the citrus aroma of her shampoo.

No need to touch her. That wasn't part of this game.

The next thing Bob knew she shoved her chair back hard, catching him in the gut. She managed to knock his wind out and leave him gasping for breath. She stood and looked him dead in the eyes.

"Oh, I'm so sorry," she said. "I didn't know you were standing there."

Laura walked down the hall without looking back. Well, this was turning out to be a lovely day all around.

Bob walked back into his office, rubbing what would surely be a bruise just under his sternum. As was often the case, the resulting bad mood let him get a lot more work done on the presentation than he would have otherwise.

Bob jumped when his phone rang through several hours later, only then realizing he'd worked long past the time he usually left for the day. He cursed the new central phone system that even super-techy Laura couldn't manage to forward to voice mail.

"What is it?"

"Mr. Henderson? This is Drew Adams, in Building Services. I need to speak to you. Do you have a few minutes?"

"My assistant handles all building issues on our floor, and no I don't."

"This concerns you directly, and I wouldn't be calling so late if it wasn't important. We need to talk now, Mr. Henderson. Subbasement level two, fourth door on the right."

Bob snorted. That officious little geek had actually hung up on him. Presentation or not, he was going to straighten this bullshit out right now.

He got up slowly, stretching out legs and back that had taken a set after sitting still for so long before he opened the door.

"Laura…"

She was gone. Gone for the day from the looks of her dark screen and neat desk, and he still had so much to do. She'd left the data he needed stacked up in his box, sure. But she hadn't even asked if he needed anything else.

Now on top of the rest of this glorious day, Bob had no one to back him up with whatever nonsense Adams had up his craw.

Chapter 2

Bob despised the building's subbasements.

Boring as the hallways above his head were, all cloaked in varying shades of beige, at least they were predictable. Calm. Unlikely to surprise him in unpleasant ways, at least until the globes appeared.

Down here, though, any pretense at creating an environment fit for human beings had long been abandoned. Painfully bright rows of lighting ran along the middle of the ceiling unencumbered by sound damping tiles or any other covering. Bob could see straight through to the building's steel beams and endless bundles of wires and ductwork. Even without the tiles, this level was eerily silent compared to the hum of activity upstairs.

He tried to convince himself that only his earlier idea of the hallway growing eyes put bones and veins into his mind. The truth was he'd thought exactly the same thing on his only other trip down to the bowels of the building.

Another unfortunate choice of words there. The smell here wasn't quite that unpleasant, though the scent of hot plastic and the ozone odor of electricity left his head swimming. The dry, overly chilly air turned his sinuses into aching lumps in his skull.

Bob kept his eyes focused straight ahead, doing his best to ignore the walls he walked by. As if having no protection over his head wasn't enough, the passage was made up of metal racks full of electronics. Regular branches of the blue, yellow, and black wires overhead dropped down to the endless blinking mass Bob had no desire to understand. He wouldn't have touched it for any reward.

He also did his best to keep his thoughts focused straight ahead, no matter how agitated he was over the interruption. Better to think of Adams and whatever he wanted than coming down here to visit Carol.

The gorgeous, fiercely intelligent lead CBU tech who'd so shamelessly flirted with him had been motivation enough to get him down here. Furious as he'd been over the installation of the sprawling circuitry he was walking through right now, meeting Carol shifted the whole thing to positive.

She'd been motivation enough for Bob in more areas than he would have believed back then. He'd never imagined how much he'd miss her now, either.

Bob's armor of forced swagger and self-confidence, brought forward to get his mind back to the trouble at hand, lasted barely a minute once he was inside Adams's cramped office. At least there were proper walls and a ceiling, even if they were covered in diagrams and charts that looked like pure gibberish to Bob.

His discomfort with the shelves and even the floor being stuffed full of books and piles of paperwork vanished once the burly redheaded tech started talking.

"There's some kind of mistake," Bob said. "I don't print anything. That's what my assistant is there for. I only use the network for email and a calendar. That's it."

"Well, there's a problem with your email too, but let's

focus on the data you accessed," Adams said, leaning back in his chair. The desk was far too cluttered with bits of electronic junk to put his feet up. "Yesterday you printed confidential company information, then more restricted files this morning. You shouldn't have privileges to that data in the first place, but no matter how you got to it, you know better than to print things like that without authorization. I need more information from you, or I'll have to audit your use of the system during the past several weeks."

"But I don't know how to use the damn thing for any of that!" Bob gritted his teeth, hating Adams more than he hated himself for admitting his own ignorance. He had to get this back into sane territory. "I don't have a computer at home. I never have. I didn't have one with me at the meeting either. Ask Tim. Laura does all of the documents. She stores everything. She prints everything. Can't you use the camera over Laura's desk to see that I never went to the printer?"

"Cameras over…you don't mean the mirrors in the hall?" He paused to chuckle, reinforcing Bob's newly-born hatred. "Bit paranoid, aren't you? You did spend a lot of time in your office. That's what triggered the alarm: high volumes of email today after hardly any activity in the past. I have to make sure confidential information wasn't sent out to competitors. I understand you had a reduction in project funding today, but that doesn't excuse what you may have done. Not even if you're looking for another job."

"I told you I haven't done any of that! I'm not looking for another job!"

Adams sat forward, folding his hands in his lap. Bob hadn't exactly helped himself by shouting like that, but he didn't appreciate the accusations. Or the jab about being paranoid. He was beyond sick of that particular word.

"You might be if this kind of thing keeps up, Mr.

Henderson. I'm going to audit your network usage for the past month. Then we'll talk again. If this turns out to be nothing, great. I'll shake your hand and say I'm sorry. If it keeps looking like it does right now, I'll pack up your office myself. Goodnight."

Chapter 3

Carol Wilson tried her best to ignore the sequence of numbers buzzing against her wrist. Getting into a non-urgent call from a past job wasn't going to help her get this new one back on schedule. No matter how many preliminary interviews and checklists and procedures she instituted, new clients always managed to find last-minute tasks to add to her list.

One of the most common, unfortunately, had already taken up most of the afternoon and well into the evening. She tapped pause on the slender digital recorder, no longer than her pinky finger. The list of neglected but critical greetings and commands on the desk display didn't seem any shorter than when she'd started.

Finalizing the installation and getting this CBU up and running wouldn't happen without these recordings. Explaining the procedure and training the correct tone of voice with someone else would take longer than doing it herself. And almost all her clients these days demanded a human voice instead of synthetic. They swore they could tell the difference.

Carol doubted that very much. But she welcomed the nice bonus fee for such last-minute personal service.

She tilted her head toward her left shoulder, then her right. Between her tense muscles and aching throat, maybe it was time for a break, after all.

Before she managed to get out of the musty supply closet, the only place quiet enough in a busy hospital for recording, Carol groaned. If she'd been paying closer attention, she would have recognized the code for Bob's building sooner.

Ignoring the call wasn't an option, not with an ongoing support contract. Neither was calling when she was half-asleep from hours of recording. Stretching her arms toward the low ceiling, Carol marched in place for a few seconds, trying to get her blood moving.

At least the code wasn't from Bob's desk phone. She'd blocked that one the day she left him.

Carol sat back down, grabbed her work phone, and tapped to return the call. She forced herself not to hold her breath. Bob didn't seem like the type to bother calling from another desk just to annoy her. But stranger things had happened.

"Adams here."

Carol exhaled, trying not to breathe into phone's speaker.

"Hey there, Drew. Carol here. You didn't break my building already?"

"Not yet, but I'm not giving up. Sorry to bother you, everything is running great here. We're having more of a personnel problem."

Carol rubbed her eyes, trying not to groan again.

"Training isn't my area. You know that. The system has the contact information for several licensed vendors who can help with personnel problems."

"Not the kind we're having. It's Bob, Carol. He seems to be having some kind of trouble."

"Now you're really outside my area. Bob and I split. He definitely has trouble, but nothing I can solve. I doubt anyone can."

Silence on the other end had Carol hoping the call had dropped.

"I didn't know you two split. Sorry again. That might explain the way he's acting." Drew sighed loud and long. "I hate to say this, but it might affect you anyway."

Carol stood again, fighting an urge to kick the boxes of paper and pens on the bottom shelves. Who used such antiquated supplies in the age of building automation, anyway?

"I doubt it, but I do have a contract saying I'll address your concerns. What's the problem?"

By the time Drew outlined all of Bob's violations, including supposedly accessing restricted data, she was shaking her head. The surly attitude she believed without question.

Breaking into secured areas of the building's network? Not a chance.

"That just doesn't sound like him. To tell you the truth, I don't think he *could* do all of that. You sure my building isn't broken?"

Drew laughed, a great booming guffaw that got a tiny smile out of Carol.

"Running a standard diagnostic as we speak, ma'am. I'll start a deep scan when I head out here in a few minutes. With a system running this smoothly, and brand new, I don't think the malfunction is in the equipment. Not the electronic equipment."

"If you find a glitch," she said, "in the CBU, I mean, please let me know. Otherwise, I'm sure you'll find an in-house solution."

"Understood."

Carol pulled out a bottle of water out of her bag, then leaned forward, face in her hands. The last thing she needed was to get drawn back into Bob and all his…complications. A CBU specialist and the worst paranoid technophobe she'd ever heard of never had any business dating the first place, much less living together.

Still, she missed the jerk. Most of all when she was tired and stressed, like right now.

She just had to remind herself how Bob created more stress than he relieved toward the end. And keep reminding herself, however long that took.

Carol drained half the water, grabbed the recorder, and got back to work.

Chapter 4

Bob managed to drive home, park, and walk the short distance to his building without paying attention to anything on the busy city streets around him. His block was quieter than most, with solid brick buildings more than one hundred years old rather than glassy, cold high rises. Even the annoyance of parking a couple of blocks away rather than in a spacious underground garage was well worth it for the peace and quiet.

If nothing else, that lack of on-street or underground parking reduced traffic to a minimum. Smelling fresh flowers from street vendors and restaurants serving the dinner crowd beat choking on exhaust fumes every time.

Instead of enjoying his walk out of the chaotic modern city and into his preferred past, Bob's mind endlessly replayed everything that jerk Adams had said. So much so that he that he nearly walked into two muscle-bound guys lugging a blocky purple sofa out of his building.

"Trying to work here," one of the huge men said.

Bob looked up, right at a giant orange moving van. The men, dressed in overalls the same eye-searing color, were now straining to carry the sofa up a rusty metal ramp into the van. He scowled, wondering who was so desperate to get moved in or out that they'd pay sky-high evening labor rates.

Then he remembered.

"By all means, move that junk out," he said as he walked up the brick stairs. "The sooner Loony Larry's gone, the better."

Bob stopped for a second when the heavy glass doors closed behind him, taking a deep breath. Carol made fun of him for the whole thing, but that didn't matter. Certainly not any more. Getting out of the all-encompassing network made something in Bob's head relax, every single time.

He hadn't scoured the entire city looking for a building like this on some kind of whim: a last century beauty proudly not connected to the network at all. As soon as he walked into the dark wood and stone-floored lobby, his whole body felt the difference.

He felt better until the last man on Earth Bob wanted to run into after a crap day stepped out of the elevator with his head down. Bob tried to duck up the stairs to his right, figuring climbing five flights was better than a confrontation. He was too late.

"Don't worry, Bob," Larry said. "I'll be out of your Luddite paradise by the end of the day. No need to run and hide."

Bob turned on his heel and continued toward the elevator.

"I'm not running, Larry. You knew when you moved in this was an off-net building. We have every right to keep it that way."

Larry's face reddened, and Bob was certain he was dying to push the ridiculous flop of hair off his forehead. He'd watched Larry do that countless times during tenant board meetings. It was a perfect indicator that the younger man was about to lose it. Only the box he carried stopped him.

"I'll tell you one last time, you son of a bitch," Larry said, settling for flipping his head back like a woman. "This was my grandmother's place. She died. I didn't move in to try to force you knuckle-draggers into the last century. I moved in to keep my family from having to sell it. I never imagined wanting a basic network connection would turn you all into such assholes."

He walked past without another word. Bob knew he should do the same. He'd been fond of the kid's grandmother, a woman about the age of his own grandparents with a healthy distrust of the network. He knew all that, but he couldn't resist a parting shot.

"It's the damn network that makes you so crazy."

Larry stopped at the door and stared into Bob's eyes. An uneasy knot twisted his guts, and Bob was sure Larry would drop the box and charge back inside. When the elevator door creaked open, he made his escape without looking back.

Another unpleasant surprise waited just inside his apartment. Carol hadn't gotten her stack of boxes out today like she'd promised. Bob kicked two of them, more out of frustration than his path being blocked.

She was just as addicted to the network as that jackass Larry.

His brain tried to convince his heart it was just as well *she* was gone, too.

When his stomach reminded him how late he'd worked, Bob admitted one good thing about Carol living here. She'd never been able to get him to budge about automated ordering and delivery, letting the appliances and cabinets handle everything. But she at least kept food in the place. The two weeks since she left had made quite a dent in the supplies. The non-smart refrigerator and most of the cupboards were empty.

Bob picked up the phone, smiling at the old-fashioned dial tone Carol so hated. He ran his fingers along the twisty spiral cord, straightening it as he went.

It would tangle up again as soon as he let go, but a cordless didn't go with an old landline somehow.

"Famous Joe's Pizza, what can I get ya?"

"I need a large pepperoni, thick crust." Bob glanced in the fridge again. "And a six-pack of Coke."

"Sure thing. Just a second, I'm having trouble getting your name and address. It's not coming through yet."

Bob grimaced. He called often enough that the usual delivery guys knew not to ask.

"It's not going to come through. My building is off-net. Got something to write with?"

"Off-net? Really?" Bob could hear the kid's smile. "I didn't know there were any off-net buildings left."

Bob closed his eyes, considering his options. He could tell this kid to shove the pizza wherever he preferred, but he'd have to go out shopping or call in a grocery order. Either way, that would be at least another hour of his headache getting worse before he could eat. He was definitely not in any mood to go out to some restaurant by himself.

Most of all, he didn't want to cause trouble with the best pizza place anywhere nearby.

"Listen, are any of the regular delivery guys there? Just tell them it's Bob Henderson. They know where I am, and they know how well I tip."

Bob winced as the kid shouted without covering the handset. Carol had fought him even on this simple thing, insisting on using her network phone with its built-in tracking for everything.

She never learned his address, not even after basically

living with him for six months. She told him no one knew addresses anymore.

"Okay, got it. Give us about twenty minutes."

He grabbed the one of the few things in the fridge, a beer, on his way into the living room. He was too tired and hungry to drink on an empty stomach, too tense not to.

The place seemed more empty and bare than before Carol moved in, even though she hadn't taken any of his things.

"It wasn't worth it," he said as he sank into his recliner. "Too much trouble."

Before he could get nostalgic for whatever the good parts were, Bob set about reminding himself what had been so bad, especially in the end. That was one of his most successful habits.

Chapter 5

Bob jerked his foot away the second he stepped onto the deep shag rug under his coffee table. He only spilled a little of the red wine before he managed to set the two glasses down.

He was almost glad the spill had hit his t-shirt rather than Carol's pale blue rug. Almost.

A black gleam caught his eye when he sat to inspect his foot. That jab was sharp enough that Bob was certain he'd see blood. He plucked a tiny bit of plastic out of the carpet, held edge up by the deep fibers, with his fingernails.

One of Carol blasted transponders, only a few millimeters on each side, the blinking red lights glaring into Bob's skull.

He closed his eyes, willing himself to stay calm. He knew he was way out of his league with Carol, and he was afraid she'd started to figure that out for herself. They'd managed not to fight or snap at each other for two whole days. A minor miracle.

Was he really going to risk messing up the best relationship he'd ever had over a piece of stray technology smaller than the tip of his finger?

Bob focused on her humming to herself in the kitchen. She only did that when she was happy, looking forward to something as silly as cuddling with his grouchy ass on the couch to watch a movie so bad it was good. So bad that none of the net's digital services had ever carried it.

Carol had been delighted with Bob's huge collection of antique silvery discs, determined to watch every one with him.

He already smelled her outrageously good garlic and pepper popcorn.

Right. Bad movie, good company, and with any luck, great sex later on.

He dropped the transponder onto the coffee table and put his blood-free foot down, enjoying the feel of the carpet through his toes. Bob leaned forward to grab his mostly full wine glass, and froze.

Three pulsing red reflections shone against the hardwood floor beyond the rug, all coming from under one of his grandmother's antique wooden chairs. He didn't have to look back at the one on the table to know all four were blinking in unison.

"This place is turning into a tech junkyard," he said under his breath. "Or a network beacon."

"What did you just say?"

Bob turned around, unpleasantly surprised to see Carol standing in the doorway, oversized orange popcorn bowl in hand. His mouth watered from the aroma despite his contracting, angry stomach.

"I didn't know you were there."

"Yeah, I'm here." She slammed the bowl onto the coffee table hard enough to spill a pepper-speckled drift across the blue rug. "I'm not surprised you didn't know it. You might as well say it to my face, Bob. You've been saying it behind my back long enough."

Bob knew he was responding to the wrong person before he opened his mouth. He shouldn't be taking his frustration at work out on his girlfriend. Again.

Those flashing beacons, connecting themselves to gods only knew what, forced the words out anyway.

"Fine, I will. I think you've brought just about enough of your stuff over here, Carol."

She crossed her arms, and the motion drew Bob's eyes to her breasts. He'd never understood why she got offended when just looking at her turned him on, even when he was pissed at her.

"My stuff?" she said. "You don't like my *stuff*? You won't ever come over to my place. What am I supposed to do?"

"You know I'm not comfortable there."

Bob chewed the insides of his cheeks.

Just stop now. Both of us. Just stop.

"Yeah, you're not comfortable." Carol smiled, but there was nothing warm or happy about it. "I've been pretty damn understanding about that. For six months now I've just about lived over here. And now you're going to bitch about me having a few things of my own? What's bothering you so much? My hairbrush? My toothbrush? A couple of pillows? Some decent things to cook with? You're such a *guy* sometimes."

"No, it's none of that." Bob fought the urge to turn on the TV to make this conversation stop. "I'm fine with of that. I appreciate you being here, I do."

"Then what's your problem?" Carol stood over him. "Where's the mythical line of too much of my stuff that turned you into such a jerk? My clothes? The groceries I'm perfectly willing to pay for?"

"No, that's not it." Bob jumped up and walked into the

kitchen, certain this was the conversation he'd afraid of since she'd first smiled at him months ago. "Forget about it, okay?"

"I'm sick to death of this, Bob." Her voice rose as she followed him. "Either you want me here or you don't. Grow up and be honest with me!"

Bob spun around, furious with her and more with himself.

He did want her around, very much. He wasn't willing to back down on this one though.

"All that's fine, Carol. Bring more of it if you want to. Of course I want you here. I just don't want any of your networked stuff here. Is that really too much to ask?"

Her mouth dropped open. Before he could explain, she did exactly what he was afraid of.

She laughed.

"That again? Come on, this is getting to be an obsession with you! You knew what I did when we met. I was installing the CBU in *your* office building. You knew exactly who I was. And now after all the nasty little comments about my job and refusing to set foot in my apartment, after everything I'm willing to do to make this work, you throw that in my face?"

"You knew this was an off-net building! I live here for a reason, and it's not just to inconvenience you. I've wasted hours of my life at those horrible tenant board meetings trying stop this very thing."

She shook her head. "No, this is different. I understand why you did that, even if I don't agree. That was someone wanting to bring in the network, to hard wire it. My phone isn't going to rewire the whole damn building."

Bob backed up against the cool tiled counter, unable to get away without shoving past her. He was as trapped as he was by the blasted network, right here in his own apartment.

"I've found transponders here too, scattered everywhere.

The network looks around for itself! Bringing all that junk in here is the best way to-"

She snarled and jammed her fists against his chest, driving his spine painfully into the edge of the counter.

"That's it! You're crazy, Bob! A damned paranoid! We're through!"

Bob rubbed his back, trying to figure out why he'd said something so stupid to her of all people. He was fine with people knowing he didn't like the network. He wasn't alone in that.

He was not fine with anyone knowing it scared the life out of him. He shouted at the slamming front door.

"Good! Get your damn network out of here, too!"

Chapter 6

A KNOCK at his door startled Bob into spilling what was left of his beer, right down the front of his pants.

"Son of a… Hang on!"

He managed to get his wallet out and pay the guy without too much fumbling, and he tipped a couple of dollars more than he usually did.

Carol called it hush money, the price of keeping his anti-network fears secret. Bob called it self-preservation.

The smell of fresh baked crust and spicy pepperoni filled his apartment, mixing with the beer on his pants better than it had any right to. As he put the box on the counter, Bob glanced at the leak on the ceiling. The brown stain by the range hood had only been an inch or so across, but Carol noticed it. She'd complained about that too, using it as yet another dig at Bob's apartment.

Of course in her perfect little automated world, such a thing would never happen. New buildings didn't get leaks, even on the top floor. Even if older renovated ones did, they took care of themselves or automatically called in a repair crew

Bob hadn't remembered to let the superintendent know about the leak yet, and it was getting bigger, probably three or four inches and starting to sag in the middle. Just one more fantastic thing to top off this lovely day.

With the state his clothes and his mind were in, Bob decided not to bother with the Coke after all. He finished the five remaining beers along with half the pizza, slouching on the couch and ignoring the blaring television.

Carol was right about one thing.

When he got into a mood like this, Bob could obsess with the best of them.

He hated to admit it, even to himself, but the audit worried him. Adams wouldn't consider that the CBU might have malfunctioned. After all, the system was brand new, state of the art, very expensive.

That was probably the main reason Bob's projects kept getting cut. Too much money dumped into the almighty CBU.

The office now had the most modern building maintenance unit available, one of the first to combine routine maintenance and wiring with computer and phone network monitoring.

Light source defective? No problem, the building took care of it as soon as it happened. Need a room wired for an extra phone? Just have the building do it. Even better, this CBU was self-sensing for most things.

No one even had to ask.

Bob had grown up with self-reliant buildings like everyone else, but he'd never liked the idea. He imagined tiny mechanical fingers in the ceilings replacing the lights, stealthy robots doing the cleaning at night, most of the activity invisible. All of it coordinated by the central unit lurking in the subbasement.

Any technology with that much control would eventually mess something up.

He was torn between blaming the building or his assistant for the mess at work. Or maybe he could blame Carol for installing the thing and using her own voice for all the system prompts. Just one more way to torment him.

Even after she was out of his life.

No matter who he blamed, he still had the presentation in a few hours. When that was over, he'd have a few words with his assistant before Adams and his audit. No one else could have accessed that data, and she could easily figure out how to send email from his account.

Hell, she might even have his company laptop at her place right now. He'd never wanted to bring the thing home after she set it up.

Bob finally staggered into his empty bed sometime well past midnight, defenses weak enough to admit Carol had been the one good thing to come out of the disruption in his dependably routine work life. If she hadn't been there installing the CBU, back when she found his dislike of the network charming instead of infuriating, he never would have met her.

Her digital life had been such a great balance to his analog, at first.

The last fragile mental self-defense fell, and Bob couldn't deny he missed her.

He missed her voice, the organic version of it at least. He missed her skin, the smell and taste of her, her warmth in the night, everything about her.

Now even that little bit of good was gone.

Chapter 7

THIS TIME TIM showed no signs of slowing as he stepped off the elevator. Bob didn't bother trying to stop him. He lagged behind, wanting his partner to continue to his own office and close the door. Tim waited by Bob's office instead, arms crossed, tapping one foot.

"What the hell was that all about?" Tim said, following Bob inside.

"I told you, I overslept."

"Overslept, then went to the wrong place! I waited for you for two hours, Bob. Exactly what was I supposed to tell the directors while I waited for you for two hours?"

"I told you I'm sorry." Bob sat and closed his eyes. "When I left yesterday, the meeting was supposed to be here. I had no way-"

"Oh, of course. You had no way to know. I'm not the only one who's getting sick and tired of that little excuse. My building let me know first thing this morning, even adjusted my alarm so I could get there in time. Modern technology is amazing, buddy. You lost a great woman over this off-net nonsense, you've probably lost both of us a big project, and you might just lose yourself a job next."

"That was out of line, Tim," Bob said, opening his eyes and sitting forward. "There was a lot more than that going on with me and Carol."

"Was there? Steve and I had dinner with Carol last night. We had a nice, long talk. You drove a kid out of his grandmother's apartment, and you think Carol was trying to infect your precious little building somehow? Because she had a couple of transponders with her? You're losing it, man. You need to get out of that crazy paranoid place and get some help."

Tim finally stomped to his office, slamming the door behind him. The words echoed through Bob's brain, circling around until they settled on one uncomfortable fact that wasn't quite as uncomfortable as the others.

He probably *had* lost this project, for both of them. Out of everything that had gone wrong, this was one thing he could do something about.

He could try, anyway.

Bob managed to work until someone knocked, nearly four hours later. Laura opened the door without waiting for him to answer.

"Mrs. Jackson needs to speak with you."

"It's late, I'll talk to her tomorrow." Bob stretched as he stood. "I need to talk to you about the computers. I think we could do that now."

The idea made him feel a little better, even after his disastrous morning.

"No. I need to leave now. Mrs. Jackson wants to talk to you about the computers too. She's waiting."

And she was gone. Maybe he did want to talk to Mrs. Jackson after all. The HR manager might be interested in

Laura's conduct over the past few days. Not tonight, though. He had other things to do.

He wasn't sure anything was going to save this project, but he might have thought of a way to save his job.

Bob picked up the phone, wincing as Carol's voice informed him he had an urgent contact request. The system put him through without asking. Before he could say a word, Mrs. Jackson was off and running.

"Mr. Henderson, thank you for calling. I need to speak with you about a few things, but it's getting a little late this evening. I see you're available tomorrow morning at 9:30?"

"Is this about the CBU?"

"Among other things. So you can make it," a rattle of her keyboard, "and we're scheduled. See you then in my office. Good night."

Mrs. Jackson hung up without waiting for Bob to agree.

His plan couldn't wait until the next day. He needed evidence. Bob closed his door again and settled in.

When the only car he saw in the parking lot was his, Bob stepped into the deserted hallway. The lighting units had switched to the lower night setting, and all the doors he could see were closed. Good enough.

The globe over Laura's desk was at the perfect angle to see her computer. If she'd accessed the data, it would all be recorded. He could go into the meeting tomorrow knowing the globes were cameras, and he'd demand they use the recordings in his defense.

He went back to his desk for his screwdriver, an interchangeable head model his grandfather had given him years ago. Bob smelled the old man's strong coffee breath again, felt scratchy beard kisses against his cheek. The old man told an eight-year-old Bob to never trust the network, to always know how to do things for himself.

Tim and Laura and Carol and anyone who saw it teased

him about having such a thing at all, much less in an auto-mated building. Now it was going to save his ass, exactly the way Granddad said it would.

For a fleeting second, it occurred to him that anything he did now would be recorded. Well, if he had to look a little awkward to save himself, it was worth it.

The globe was just out of reach, so he rolled Laura's chair over. He stepped up slowly, bracing the chair against the wall. No fasteners, at least not visible ones.

He wedged the screwdriver along the edge of the globe and pulled.

Nothing.

He moved his free hand from the wall to the screwdriver and pulled again.

When he shifted his weight for more leverage, the chair rolled out from under him. Bob gasped and wheezed, flat on his back, trying to recover the breath he'd knocked out of his lungs.

He screamed when he put his hand down to push himself up. He'd managed to jam the screwdriver right through the meaty part just below his thumb.

Pulling it out only made the agony worse.

And still the globe revealed nothing, except maybe to whoever watched the recording.

Chapter 8

AFTER POLITE INQUIRIES about his hand, and believing his car trouble story just like the emergency room doctor had the night before, Mrs. Jackson got decidedly less polite.

Her old-fashioned flower print dress and elaborate bun hairdo clashed with an ultra-modern office loaded with moving digital photos of pets and children. Bob couldn't stand to look anywhere but into her eyes. The whole room stank of whatever was in the vile green smoothie sitting on her desk.

"Sexual harassment? I've never even touched Laura."

Squeeze.

"No," Mrs. Jackson said. "But you do have a habit of making her uncomfortable and intimidating her. I wouldn't be quite so concerned about this if there hadn't been several other problems over the past few weeks."

"What, that nonsense about the computers? That's probably why Laura is claiming harassment, to cover her tracks about whatever she printed."

Squeeze.

"I have the records right here, Mr. Henderson. This

proves you accessed the data, from here and from elsewhere. It also confirms the email messages that alerted Mr. Adams, and the phone calls that alerted the phone system. You've made several long personal calls from your office phone."

Mrs. Jackson folded her hands over the paperwork and looked at him. Bob knew she was waiting for a response, but anything he said would sound defensive at this point.

He squeezed his bandaged hand again. The pain cleared his head and calmed him down.

He hadn't noticed the blood soaking through.

"If you would just get the recordings from those damn cameras, we could straighten all this out. I don't use a computer outside this place. Laura has the code to my office door. She's usually there before I am in the mornings. She probably took my laptop home a long time ago. I don't care what those building reports say I did. Either Laura did it or the building is malfunctioning."

"Yes, Mr. Adams mentioned your confusion about cameras." Mrs. Jackson pursed her pale pink lips, then shook her head. "The globes are mirrors, nothing more. The building's security and monitoring systems are fine. They're only a few months old, and the CBU calibrated and checked everything overnight. Now, Laura has never had any trouble like this in the past-"

"Neither have I!"

Squeeze.

"...whereas you have had several problems in the past few days. I'd like to help. I know you just had a bad breakup, but some of these issues are getting too serious. Especially with your attitude this morning."

"I am going to defend myself against this bullshit!" Bob slammed his hands on the chair arms. He barely managed to keep a straight face. That pain was too much. "You can't expect me to accept everything you're accusing me of without putting up a fight. And I *will* put up a fight."

Mrs. Jackson stared at him again, then turned to her computer.

"Just in case we had this kind of discussion, I checked everyone's schedules. We're all available for a meeting tomorrow morning at eight."

"Who? Who else is mixed up in this?"

"I will be there, as will Mr. Adams, Tim Jones, and your manager. Laura will probably not attend, though I will inform her. I suggest you spend the time calming yourself and thinking about possible solutions."

She leaned forward, a perfectly concerned expression on her face. Bob wondered how long she'd rehearsed it.

"In fact, take the rest of today off. Go home and think it over. I'll make sure this doesn't count against your vacation days. I hope we can still help with whatever is going on, Mr. Henderson. But don't think for one second this isn't serious."

She turned back to the screen. Meeting over. Bob left without a word.

He never noticed the smear of blood on the chair arm or the beaded drops on the floor.

Mrs. Jackson didn't either.

They faded away before she turned around.

Chapter 9

CAROL RECOGNIZED the buzzing code right away this time. Instead of huddled in a closet recording an endless series of system messages, she was happily neck deep in CBU. Only one of the airport's several units, in fact, each several times larger than the one in Bob's building.

She traced the arm-thick bundles overhead with her eyes, comparing the team's progress with the schematic in her mind. They were a well-trained bunch after several years working with Carol. As usual, they'd kept everything moving while she dealt with the typical front end delays on such a huge project.

Plenty of time for a good-natured chat with Drew Adams, maybe about the relative size of their current CBUs.

Maybe find out if their personnel problem was resolved.

Carol climbed down the ladder out of the subbasement ceiling, waving to her lead tech before she stepped into the elevator lobby. The unmistakable chemical reek of jet fuel crept in even way down here. Drew picked up on the first ring.

"That airport job must be easier than it sounds if you have time to chat with a small-timer like me."

"The first three units weren't bad," she said. "The next eight might be more of a challenge."

Drew whistled. "Maybe you can sneak an old buddy down there sometime. I'd love to see that. Listen, I know you're just humoring me, so I'll get right to it. Bob's getting worse, Carol."

She paced in the long, narrow room, covering her eyes with one hand.

"Worse how? Not more with the building systems?"

"I don't know, maybe. HR wouldn't say much, but they'll calling me and a bunch of other people into a meeting first thing in the morning. Word is he's demanding we review the video from those cameras in the hall. To prove his innocence."

"That again? Where is this even coming from?"

Carol leaned against the cool cinderblock wall. She had her suspicions. Or at least her guilt.

"He's always been weird about tech," Drew said. "You know that. But he's never had this kind of trouble before. Bitching and moaning about the network is one thing. If any of the CBU's reports are true, he's trying to get fired or hurt the company somehow."

"I know the answer before I ask, but have you run diagnostics? It's unusual with such a new system, but there could be some kind of problem."

Drew snorted. "In one you set up? Not hardly. And yeah, I checked everything over the past couple of days. Running perfect, no glitches. Still, like you said. This doesn't make sense. Not from Bob."

Carol drew in a sharp breath when her wrist unit buzzed again. That was the code for this job, not some ex come back to haunt her.

She might wonder if she had something to do with Bob's breakdown or whatever it was in the back of her mind. Whether she'd pushed him over some kind of truly phobic edge she'd had no way to know was real.

But she still had work to do here. Right now.

"I'm sorry, Drew, I've got to get back in there. I don't...I don't think it sounds like Bob, either. Let me know how the meeting goes tomorrow?"

"Sure. I'm running the diagnostic audit of his system usage right now. If this all does turn out to be some kind of glitch, you'll be the first person I call."

"I'd better be. Thanks, Drew. Take care."

Chapter 10

BOB SLAMMED HIS APARTMENT DOOR, too angry to remember to step over the boxes in the entry. He stopped his fall with his injured hand.

He sucked air in through his teeth and curled his hand up against his chest, staring at the blood smearing the pale tan wall.

"Damn it, Carol! I told you to get this junk out of here!"

He stumbled through to the kitchen, flipping the light switch with his elbow. Once he managed to pull the blood-soaked dressing off, Bob grunted.

Two of the stitches had pulled loose. The other three held, but the wound on his palm wasn't closed anymore. The back of his hand was red and swollen, but the sutures were fine.

He dropped the blood stinking pile in the garbage and headed toward the bathroom.

By the time he finished the incredibly awkward task of wrapping up his own hand, Bob was good and angry. He wasn't sure what he was so furious with, but he had plenty of targets to choose from.

He opened the medicine cabinet to put the bandages back, and his gaze fell on the empty shelf. The space he'd cleared out so Carol would have somewhere to leave her precious stuff.

Target locked on. Proceed with rage.

Back in the kitchen, he dialed her number. He wondered for a second if she'd bother to answer, then remembered the pizza kid's confusion.

Yep, off-net buildings still existed. And a network phone had no idea who was calling from one.

"Hello? Who's calling please?"

"I told you to get your crap out of here, and you promised you would days ago. What the hell is the holdup?"

"Bob. Good to hear your voice, too. I've been busy the past week, installing the new CBU at the airport. You knew that was coming up."

"And you know these boxes are in my way here."

"Hey, if it's bothering you so much, take them downstairs. Roger will keep them for me."

"You don't live here, Carol. You don't even visit anymore. The super has more than enough to do without keeping up with your junk."

Bob glanced toward the entry and forgot all about Carol. He forgot about the boxes.

He forgot about everything but that pale paint on the wall.

That completely clean wall.

He jumped when she spoke again.

"Just kick it out in the hall, then, I don't care! I'm busy here. If we can wrap this part up tonight, I'll try to stop by. As a matter of fact, just put it out there now. I'd rather someone steal all of it than have to see you!"

She ended the call, but Bob couldn't speak anyway. He was too busy staring at the wall.

He remembered exactly how the blood looked, like an afterimage on his retinas. He remembered exactly how hitting the wall felt.

He looked down at his re-bandaged hand, then hung up the phone and walked over to the garbage can on numb legs that never seemed to touch the floor.

The disgusting bandages were still there.

The blood on the counter was still there.

Wasn't it?

Bob bent down, squinting at the smooth tiles.

Going, going, gone.

His mouth dropped open as the last drop disappeared, sinking into the stone.

Bob backed up, heart pounding in his ears, looking wildly around his apartment.

He could not have imagined that. He'd gotten his own blood on the paint and on the counter, and now it was gone.

No. This was not possible.

He bumped against the opposite wall and jumped away as if it were burning hot.

The wall, the damn wall had dissolved his blood some-how, soaked it in. Even in a networked building, he'd never heard of such a thing.

And this was no networked building.

"Paranoid," he whispered, walking slowly toward the phone. "You're just being paranoid, buddy."

His good hand shook as he reached out. Bob was terrified the reassuring old-fashioned dial tone would be gone and he'd hear Carol's voice instead, asking how she could help him. He touched the handset for a moment before he finally picked it up.

He let out his breath in a whoosh when he heard the familiar churning buzz. He cradled the handset on his shoulder and dialed with his left hand.

"Roger here."

"Roger. This is Bob Henderson up on five. I'm having a little trouble here."

"What's going on, Bobby H?"

Roger's annoying habit of using the same absurd nickname for every tenant didn't even bother Bob. He barely heard it.

His eyes locked on to the leak in the ceiling again.

It was much bigger than the day before, and sagged several inches lower.

"Bob?"

"I… uh…there's a leak up here, Roger. A leak. A bad one."

Bob backed up as far as he could, the stretched cord nearly pulling the phone out of his hand. The leak didn't look nearly so random and accidental as it had just a couple of weeks ago. It didn't look like it had a few hours ago either.

It looked regular.

Round.

Planned.

"Sure thing, I'll be up in a couple of hours. You don't have water coming through now, do you?"

"No, no. No water coming through. Soon as you can, Roger, okay? Soon as you can."

"No problem, Bobby H. See you in a bit."

Bob dropped the phone, the recoiling cord twisting and spinning it across the tile floor. He backed slowly toward the hall closet, never taking his eyes off of the thing in the kitchen.

That thing was shaped too much like those globes all over his office building. He reached inside and got out a broom, yet another antiquated tool Carol laughed at.

Bob couldn't imagine laughing at anything right now.

"You think you'll take my blood?" He moved forward,

the broom handle held up like a sword. "My fucking blood? You'll have to take all of it."

He got as close as he could without touching the range that now seemed like a demon waiting to pull him inside and roast him alive.

Bob leaned up, pushing the handle against the thing on his ceiling. It sunk in at first, just like it should have.

Then it touched something hard.

He tapped. It sounded like glass.

Bob took a deep breath, and he hit the thing as hard as he could. The coating fell away as the glass shattered, revealing a small camera underneath.

The camera turned for a few seconds, scanning the room, before it locked onto Bob.

He heard the faint whine as the lens focused.

"Robert Paul Henderson, your damage of network property has been recorded."

A woman's voice, Carol's voice, from the tiny camera.

"Action will be taken."

Bob screamed, dropping the broom as he turned to run.

His feet tangled in the spiraling phone cord and he fell heavily. His forehead made a loud, wet crack against the floor.

Blood in his eyes kept him from seeing anything else.

But right before he blacked out, Bob's ears worked perfectly.

He heard the camera, still focusing.

He heard the same voice coming from the phone's handset.

Carol's voice followed Bob into oblivion.

"Emergency services will arrive momentarily."

Chapter 11

Carol stood in the creaky, ancient elevator, gripping the railing with her eyes closed. She'd hated the thing when she still had a reason to come here.

Now the musty, swaying box felt like a shrinking cage.

It finally jerked to a stop, and she darted out as soon as she could squeeze through the doors.

She was digging in her pack for the old-fashioned key, the only one she had, when voices caught her attention. She slowed, thinking they were coming from Bob's apartment.

Sure enough, the voices got louder as she turned the corner.

"I don't care who you think called you, I didn't let you in!"

Carol was certain she recognized that voice, though she'd never heard him shouting before.

"Roger? Bob! What happened?"

Three EMTs in their official gray network uniforms glanced at her, then turned back to the man on the floor.

Bob. Unconscious, blood pooling around his head.

"Careful in here, Carol," Roger said, walking toward her.

"Not sure how he managed it. Cracked his head pretty good. I don't know what the hell *they're* doing here either."

"We keep telling you," the lead tech said, scowling. "The building called and reported the emergency. It's standard procedure, certainly when someone's unconscious."

"And I'm telling you this building isn't wired," Roger said, fists clenched. He relaxed them as he turned to Carol. "You work with these people. Back me up here?"

"He's right." She focused on the EMTs, doing her best not to look at Bob. "That's why he lives here. Not a single link in the place."

The uniformed woman shook her head.

"You'll want to double-check that, ma'am. The phone is online, and that camera is too. I thought I recognized your voice from the new hospital CBU. If you install these things, you know better than anyone we didn't get here by accident."

Carol picked up the phone, expecting the irritating buzzing dial tone.

Instead she heard her own voice.

"CBU here. How may I help you?"

She hung up and backed away, shaking her head.

Bob would never have allowed this. Never.

She'd never met anyone as loudly opposed to the network, all the way to his bones.

Roger waved one big hand toward the ceiling.

"Know anything about that?"

She followed his gaze and gasped. A tiny camera was tucked away, nearly hidden between the ventilation hood and the wall. One of the newest models, the ones they'd only started installing about six months ago.

"How long has that been here?" she said.

Roger grunted. "Never seen it. Bob never mentioned anything like that. He called me about a leak, but these jerks were here already. They let themselves in."

The woman looked up from her tablet, sighing.

"I'm sorry to keep arguing with you, but the building called us. When we get an emergency call, we have the obligation to respond. Isn't that true, ma'am?"

Carol nodded, but she didn't want to be put on the spot like this.

Nothing was making sense.

She didn't want to be here at all.

"I'll just…I'll get my things and get out of your way." Carol turned away, afraid the combined reek of blood and antiseptics was going to make her sick. She picked up her boxes and glanced back at the EMTs. "Is he going to be okay?"

"We think so, once we get him stabilized. We're taking him downtown to the brain trauma center. You just upgraded the CBU on that one a couple of months ago, didn't you?"

Carol nodded again, backing out of the apartment.

Bob was stubborn and paranoid and sometimes a real pain in the ass, but she hated to see him hurt.

She'd never wanted to leave him in the first place.

She jabbed the cracked plastic button for the elevator with her elbow.

The door opened right away. She put the boxes down, opening one and fumbling inside. She needed to blow her nose before she made a real mess of herself. The harsh buzz startled her, and she remembered she had to push another button for the floor she wanted.

"Antiquated piece of shit," she whispered, pushing the L button.

Carol saw something odd in the box then.

Something blinking.

She picked up a tiny black transponder, smaller than her

pinkie fingernail. She must have dropped it one day after work.

She'd dropped more than one, according to Bob. He was probably right.

Her sharp eyes had no trouble with the minuscule code on one side: the CBU install for Bob's office building.

She turned it over and looked closer, reading the red text that scrolled across a few characters at a time.

"Link established. Configuration in progress."

KARI KILGORE

AUTHOR OF RESTRICTED SPECIES AND THE BECALMED

THE GARBAGE BELT

For my Papaw, Arthur Kilgore

Who would decide a thing needed doing,
then work out his own unique and often
puzzling way to get it done.

And somehow, it worked.
Every single time.

Chapter 1

THERE HAD BEEN a time when Gayle Simmons would have been thrilled to pilot a brand new, state-of-the-art scouter shuttle.

Every millimeter of the compact ship gleamed. The holographic instrument display floating under her fingertips, responsive enough to know what control cluster she needed before she did. The broad expanse of the forward viewport, so transparent and flawless she would have sworn she could reach right through it. The plush command chair that cradled her whole body, adjusting to her as she moved, far more comfortable than any piece of furniture she'd ever owned.

No detail had been overlooked, no expense spared in the design of *The Treasure Hunt*. Instead of typical steel floors, walls, and ceilings, every surface of the scouter was lined with heavy charcoal grey fabric.

It had taken Simmons a few days to get used to eerie silence rather than echoing footsteps as she moved through the ship. The lining damped every single sound she, her long-time crew member Rog, or the vessel itself made.

The stuff even repelled stains somehow. Or maybe it absorbed them and turned them into money.

These days the biggest thrill Simmons got from the *Treasure* was the greatly improved odds of bringing in treasure of her own.

Only a person with more money than sense would have designed a scouter more luxurious than the finest hotel on Earth, then hired a flinty space rat like Simmons to pilot it.

She took a long swallow of nutri-stim, smiling despite her grouchy mood as the minty, sweet liquid warmed her throat and belly. No trace of metallic or chemical undertaste, not on the pride of Jamison Wyatt's private scouter fleet. Simmons was happy to take advantage of such high quality supplies when she could get them.

Outside that gorgeous viewport floated the biggest garbage dump humans had yet devised. Once fast-jump transport within the solar system became common reality about thirty years before Simmons was born, people immediately looked for a way to mark the new neighborhood as their own.

The most reliable clue to human settlement had always been vast piles of garbage. From bones to plastic to spent electronics, people never could manage to clean up after themselves.

Nowadays, humans recycled an incredible amount and used most of the rest for fuel. Not nearly as much ended up in these off-world dumps. Still, some things were too dangerous to leave floating around. And someone needed to clean up the mess already out there.

Most of the debris remained in an orderly orbit between the asteroid belt and Jupiter just like it was supposed to. Without magnification, Simmons could see dozens of dull metallic containment pods in every size and shape imaginable.

A few massive enough to hold tens of thousands of people instead of acres of their garbage were still left from the old days, along with many smaller modern versions. The smallest, only a couple of meters in diameter, usually held especially toxic waste.

Humanity took a depressingly long time to learn how to manage resources that were limited, too. They tossed out the useless and plentiful along with the rare and precious. More of that second category than most folks would have believed ended up endlessly circling out here in the ass-end of nowhere.

All things rare and precious were *The Treasure Hunt's* prey.

Simmons fired her port thrusters in a two-second burst, bringing the scouter within a few kilometers of the most likely candidate she'd seen in a sector full of useless junk. Collisions did happen out here, though usually the containers stood up to the impact. At least a couple in this vicinity had not.

Clouds of waste, some no bigger than a shoe, swirled around the space, passing through the ship's bright forward lights. A lot of the loose stuff was much larger, though, with no way to know what was truly dangerous until it was too late. Hazardous work most pilots weren't willing to do, even with pulse fields around the scouters to keep the smallest junk away.

That meant serious prizes for the few who had the guts.

The target cylinder tumbled end over end, flashing purple and black slash marks for lab-created elements. Garbage haulers a few decades ago reluctantly agreed to use that much of an identifying mark, but only for whole families of dangerous waste. Simmons was going to have to get closer to the thing to make sure it was Element 127.

Wyatt paid for just about any rare element she brought

in. The few discarded caches of 127 were the major prize she was hunting for. Not nearly enough to buy her a vessel as fine as the *Treasure*. Buying herself out of debt provided more than enough incentive.

A gusty sigh behind Simmons gave her barely a second of warning.

A carefully bored and disinterested voice said, "That at least looks promising."

Simmons leaned her shoulder to the right, then let the chair take over and rotate away from the viewport.

The only person she'd ever been able to tolerate on a mission longer than a day filled most of the oval doorway. Rog stood a few hands taller than Simmons, and his broad shoulders and strong back did help with trouble on some of the rust buckets she piloted. On a beauty like the *Treasure*, his best asset was a head like a top-notch onboard data system.

Simmons trusted her own navigational instinct to lead them to the best find in any garbage pile. She trusted Rog and his vast memory of history to know what the hell they'd found.

"Got a strong hunch it's 127," she said.

Rog raised his eyebrows.

"Been looking for that long enough. Rumor is there aren't many left out here."

"Exactly. Wyatt will pay whatever the hell we ask if we bring one in."

She turned back to the viewport and called up the external camera. Catching the ID number was tricky with the suspect spinning in the mess of ruptured containers. Sometimes a digital still image she could zoom in on worked.

"What's that gap over there?" Rog pointed up and to the right.

Simmons followed his finger toward the top of the viewport. A blank space in the swirling muddle. She frowned.

A clear area in the middle of so much junk was understandable. No different than currents and eddies on waterways of Earth. But a perfectly round area without a speck of debris, with no gravitational or geographical reason for it? That didn't fit. Nowhere in nature, not even out here in the void.

"That gap shouldn't exist," Simmons said under her breath.

She nudged the ship a bit closer, making sure she didn't lose sight of the purple and black container. She wasn't the kind of stupid to lose sight of the real prize while chasing some goofy anomaly.

A scatter of glittering junk caught in the scouter's lights, heading away from the tumbling container Simmons suspected was 127. Then the junk…curved. She couldn't see any rhyme or reason for it, but the clump of sparkling bits gradually shifted direction and thinned out.

Just as Simmons thought the change reminded her of soap bubbles swirling down a drain, the debris curved even further. Toward the blank space.

The junk disappeared.

Simmons stared, vaguely aware her mouth was hanging open but unable to do anything useful about it.

The blank space in the garbage field had simply *eaten* something. Taking it right out of reality as far as she could tell. Rog's overly loud voice jarred her back into motion.

"What the hell just happened?"

Chapter 2

All Simmons could manage to do was shake her head, but she did close her mouth. She brought the *Treasure's* sensor array online for a full scan. The unknown was most unwelcome in her line of work.

"Nothing I've ever seen before," she said. "Anything come up in that big brain of yours?"

"Forget it." Rog leaned closer to the instrument display. "I'm not saying a word until we know more."

Data scrolled across the screen before Simmons could force her mind to make sense of it. The system on any scouter automatically tried to identify and analyze objects close by. *The Treasure Hunt*, of course, sent back constantly updated results in an instant.

Simmons doubted the readings anyway.

"That can't be right," she said. "Whatever draws the junk in doesn't read as gravity. No spin, nowhere near enough mass."

Rog leaned forward and touched the screen. "Some kind of field is active, though. Almost like a tractor beam."

Simmons scowled, resisting the urge to shove him away.

She'd cut her piloting teeth on a couple of junkers that relied on beam tech. Their scarred and beat up hulls, not to mention rare successful hauls, showed just how poorly those old scouters worked.

"Tell me what's projecting it, then. If there were any kind of spacecraft within a million kilometers of here, I would have known about it hours ago."

"Hang on, there's more that doesn't make sense. I'm seeing elements that can't be out here, not without some kind of processing." He tapped the screen several times, minimizing the gravitational readings and pulling up a chemical analysis. "They show up right around the edge of your tractor beam, then they decay and dissipate."

"No one even knows what kind of junk is out here," Simmons said. She watched the readings rise close to the gap and drop off toward the edge. "Anything could be causing that."

"That's just it, Simmons. Only a few things can do that kind of processing, taking in one thing and changing it to another. Tech inside a lab, if there were one out here. Same with a star. But all we have is a gap in space that's eating junk. You're not going to like it, but that looks like a digestion plume to me."

Simmons leaned to her right, not caring that Rog had to jump back from the turning command chair.

"Digestion. You expect me to believe some kind of *creature* has set up housekeeping out here?"

Rog crossed his arms, drumming his fingers on his biceps. She knew she was getting on his nerves by keeping him away from the console, and she didn't care.

"I don't expect you to believe anything yet, not until I know more. I'm just telling you how this hole in space is acting. Think about it."

He pushed on her chair until it spun forward, then

tapped the panels. He zoomed in on the impossible elements Simmons most wanted to ignore.

"We saw garbage disappear into whatever this thing is. Those elements never occur in nature, kind of like our prize 127. They only exist within that digestion plume, not one meter beyond it. It's taking in one thing and transforming it to something else. There's no lab and there's no star. See anything else out here that could be doing that?"

"You know as well as I do there's nothing else out here. Explain it then, genius. You're always telling me about some crazy new tech or discovery you've heard of. Take a guess."

"I can tell you what it acts like." He straightened, stepping away from her chair. "They're not supposed to exist. Not this small, anyway."

"What's not, Rog? What sits out here in the middle of nowhere eating garbage and turning it into elements that can't be here?" Something tickled at the back of her mind, but she couldn't catch it.

"If I didn't see that digestion plume," he said, "I'd believe we were looking at a black hole."

Simmons rubbed her temples, trying to soothe her pounding head.

"Tell me you don't mean the things at the center of the galaxy. Black holes eat *stars*, Rog."

"Sure, the big ones do. They've thought micro black holes exist for a couple hundred years now. The theory is one this small would only last the blink of an eye. That theory could be focused on the wrong thing altogether. Maybe micro black holes are whatever this is instead. Nobody's ever seen one. We might be the first."

A container about the size of a hovercar back on Earth drifted toward the blank space. The organic black hole. Simmons gasped when the container broke up into a stream of smaller pieces. Just as before, the cloud of junk gradually curved away from its original path, thinned out, and disappeared.

"I'll be damned." Simmons switched the display to the external camera and zoomed in. "It may not be gravity, but something is pulling junk in. I can't see anything behind it."

"That kind of makes sense. Nothing gets out of a black hole. Not nearby, anyway. There's nowhere near enough discharge in that plume for what it's eaten in the last few minutes. Not enough mass to be absorbing that much volume, either. We're not seeing part of it."

"Maybe it uses all the rest?" Simmons said. "More efficiently than we do?"

"Anything that eats has to excrete. The volumes don't match up. Has to go somewhere, though. Astrophysicists think big black holes may exhaust thousands of light years away. Maybe in another dimension. Our little critter here may do the same on a smaller scale."

They watched in silence as several more loose bits of garbage drifted too close and winked out of existence.

"Do you think it will get bigger?" Simmons said. "Are we safe here?"

He shrugged. "I wouldn't even want to guess. Is it full-sized? Still growing? We're way beyond even the most exotic theories, Gayle. People haven't made it outside our solar system, much less to the center of the galaxy. We won't for a long damn time. I wasn't kidding earlier. We're probably the first to actually see whatever this is."

"Is it anchored there? It doesn't seem to be moving."

Rog shook his head and squatted beside her, eyes fixed on the hole in space.

"If it actually is alive, it would probably drift in search of food. The smallest microorganisms do that much without any kind of a brain. I'm not a biologist or physicist, just a geek who reads a lot. Wonder how long it lives? Or how much garbage it's swallowed?"

Simmons blinked, no longer seeing the hole or anything else outside her head. Her brain slipped into overdrive, yanking most of her body along with it.

"Yeah. How much garbage it can swallow is an interesting question." She turned to Rog. "How strong are the containment fields on those new canisters?"

"The shielded ones?" Rog knew her too well. His slow smile made it clear just how fast his mind was working to catch hers. "They're designed to compress and hold anything dangerous we find out here. Radiation, unstable elements. I doubt anyone was planning for living black holes."

"Even if we could catch it, could we safely move it? Something that pulls these huge garbage tankers in and devours everything in its path?"

Rog tilted his head back and forth, mouth compressed.

"We've outcompeted everything on Earth that wanted to eat us. If we did manage to capture it, *if*, we should be able to move it. Very, very carefully. Since theory is all we have to go on, remember how I said black holes this small are supposed to be unstable?"

"What do they think happens to them?" Even though none of the *Treasure's* safety systems were out of the green, Simmons fought an urge to jet them away from this sector.

"Radiation burst and explosion. Could happen to our creature here, too, if we damage or upset it. Not a pleasant way to spend an afternoon. Or, we get too close trying to catch the thing, and we manage to become its latest meal."

Numbers flashed through Simmons's mind nearly too fast to catch. The desperate need to get rid of humanity's rapidly accumulating junk created this vast wasteland in the first place. And people like Wyatt who figured out how to make it happen accumulated vast fortunes in the process.

If she and Rog could work this out, she'd be able to buy a hundred scouters as nice as *The Treasure Hunt*. A thousand. They'd eventually make the whole damn business of scouting obsolete, but not until after reaping rewards Jamison Wyatt could only dream about.

"Listen, do you have someone you could talk to about this?" she said. "Someone in your geek circles who could figure it out? Didn't scientists contain antimatter a long time ago?"

Rog stood and crossed his arms.

"I'm sure I could find somebody. Are we talking partner, someone we can trust to help us? I don't have near the expertise to build something like that."

"Well, maybe not *full* partner," she said. "More like someone we could pay off enough to keep quiet. Really quiet."

"Or else we feed them to our pet black hole?"

Rog grinned, and Simmons knew he was going to work this out no matter what it took.

"You got it, Rog. Let's set our beacons, make sure we can find our way back. Then we'll grab that cylinder back there, the one that brought me over here in the first place."

"A haul of 127 would probably pay for whatever containment we need," he said. "Assuming it's even possible."

"I trust you and your supergeek friends." Simmons launched the first set of beacons, designed to broadcast only when they detected her personal code sequence. "If this works, we can make it worth their while a thousand times over and have plenty left for ourselves."

Chapter 3

IN THE END, a little over half the paycheck for the 127 did the trick. Rog found three physics graduate students who'd crossed more lines than even Simmons was willing to, or so he claimed. He never would tell her what they'd done. Or tried to do. Something serious enough to get them to design and build the container, take the money, and disappear.

Serious enough that they accepted Rog's specs without asking one question about what this device was supposed to capture.

Simmons doubted what they eventually delivered would work to hold water, much less their creature. The so-called trap that showed up in her salvage warehouse looked like an overgrown drinking glass. Twenty meters tall and seven meters across, the material was thin enough to be nearly transparent.

The kids who designed it swore all the strength came from the banks of machinery and circuits stowed alongside the fragile-looking cylinder. The force field was what counted, they said, what would perform the engineering feat of capturing and holding a ravenous organic black hole.

They had been willing to wait for full payment until Simmons and Rog headed back out, six months after they first discovered the odd hole in space. Half up front, half wired when the capture was complete. If everything went wrong, those kids would probably be long gone and unreachable by the time they returned. Simmons tried not to think about the amount of money already spent.

If this worked, SimRog Disposal, Ltd., would earn that much in an hour for watching an insatiable space stomach do all the work.

As they approached the right sector in the garbage field, Simmons had to fight back the urge to snap at Rog. He'd been pacing behind her command chair for the last hour. Turned out even silent pacing on a luxurious sound-damping carpet was maddening as hell.

Simmons was thankful all over again that Wyatt had hired them out on *The Treasure Hunt* so soon after their last success. Neither she nor Rog would mind one bit to bring home another lucrative catch for Wyatt along with their pet black hole. And she didn't know of another scouter she'd trust for such a tough catch.

She couldn't remember feeling anxious enough for her hands to shake on a mission, not even on her first time out. This time, though, she was sure Rog spotted the tremble when she triggered their beacon code. No mission had ever come close to this dangerous, or had a chance of such mind-blowing profits.

If the beacons had failed, or if the creature had drifted, they might never find it again. Agitate the thing too much before, during, or after capture, and they might find out if the theories about instability were true. And of course, if they got too close, they'd drag Wyatt's expensive toy along with themselves into digestive oblivion.

Normal mission risks of collision or contamination from

toxic waste weren't in the same nightmare-inducing neighborhood as being eaten alive.

After the longest ten-second wait of her life, Simmons heard the answering ping of the beacons. Rog let out a breath hard enough to stir the hair on her arms, but she was too relieved to care.

"That's the easy part out of the way," he said. "Time for the miracle."

Simmons brought the controls for the external arms up on the display, then glanced at the palm-sized panel Rog held. The simplest thing in the world, the students said. Get the trap behind the creature, around it if possible, then fire the capture sequence. The rest will take care of itself.

"Think we can trust those kids, Rog?"

"Too late to turn back now. Bring it in just like any other catch. You got this."

The scouter's autopilot locked onto the beacons, bringing the *Treasure* closer while avoiding the largest debris. Simmons stared out the viewport until her eyes ached, trying to catch the blank spot in the middle of kilometers of garbage.

"There!" she said, slapping at the override for the autopilot.

The bright exterior lights showed a much larger empty space than before, but the edges were just as round and unnatural. Simmons brought them closer than the first time. Barely a kilometer away. No spikes on the ship's gravity field sensors so far, the best thing they had to stay clear of the creature's pull. She switched to a full sensor scan.

"It's the same size and mass as before," she said. "Despite a steady diet of junk. If it *has* grown, the difference is too small to detect."

"So we know it can absorb a hell of a lot of junk and stay manageable. Assuming it's manageable now."

Simmons grinned up at him, her whole body flushing hot and tingly.

"Time we found out. Launching the trap."

The display switched to external cameras aimed at the cargo bay. Simmons watched the robotic arms shifting the delicate cylinder into space, trying not to hold her breath. The scouter's full pulse field only extended ten meters beyond the hull. After that, the much weaker field attached to the trap itself would have to be enough.

"Firing remote boosters," she said.

Just like on any scouting mission, bringing the ship itself close to their target was far too dangerous. After the era of the failed tractor beams ended, even the cheapest, most outdated scouter carried miniature boosters and sleds to avoid the collision problem. Several of the fist-sized boosters and a few remote sensors would have to handle the job.

She turned the transparent cylinder so the open end faced her, ignoring all her years of experience telling her to do the opposite. Neither she, Rog, nor the students who'd designed their trap could work out how to capture something that was most dangerous from the front, even in theory.

If they were lucky, it wouldn't have enough sensory abilities to know they were coming. Simmons wasn't willing to find out with her own skin. Swinging around behind it was the only possible way.

Nine hundred meters. Seven-fifty.

"Any spikes on that pull field?" Rog said. Simmons had never heard him sounding so tense.

"None so far."

She took her time and pushed the trap far to the left of the hole, making sure she aimed well clear of the empty area. A tiny space around the cylinder pushed small debris out of the way. Everything moved at a glacial pace, even slower than a typical capture.

The display panel in front of Simmons pinged, making her and Rog jump.

"There's the pull," she said, leaning forward. "In front and off to the side, sweeping back. That's as close as I can get."

Rog nodded, fingers flying over his small panel.

"That's what the kids thought might happen. Everything curves around a black hole unless it gets pulled in. Our creature acts just like one so far. Activating trap field."

Nothing changed on the viewport in front of Simmons. She only knew the big machinery back in the cargo bay was firing up by a series of chimes from Rog's panel.

In theory, the machines and the fragile looking trap would combine to make a stronger field than antimatter containers back on Earth. In theory, as long as they avoided the danger zone right in front of the organic black hole, Simmons would be able to maneuver the trap close enough to capture it. In theory, she and Rog would safely anchor the whole rig outside the *Treasure*, then tow it outside the garbage belt.

SimRog Disposal would be born.

Simmons did not particularly like theories, not with an operation this risky. If the reward weren't potentially so great, she would have never wanted to be the one testing so many things that had only been simulated before.

In simulations, a wandering hunk of garbage almost never came up from behind.

Chapter 4

WHILE MOST OF the containers orbiting in empty space behaved and stayed in their orbits, once in a while collisions did happen. Sometimes the containers burst, sometimes not. A swirl of debris would have been a hell of a lot easier to deal with than an intact square block moving in the wrong direction.

Simmons swore when the harsh buzzer ripped through the silent cabin.

"Proximity alert," Rog said. "Where the hell did that come from?"

"The pulse field deflected it."

The exterior cameras tracked a silvery mass five meters on each side slowly detouring around the back of the *Treasure*. The display plotted a new trajectory.

Directly toward their glittering, fragile trap.

"Will it withstand impact?" Simmons said. "Does the trap's containment field work that way?"

"How should I know? I didn't design the damn thing."

Simmons forced herself to speak quietly when she wanted to yell.

"We've got about seven minutes to figure it out."

"What do you want me to do, Simmons? Suit up and go out and get it by hand?"

Simmons tried to focus, to force her mind to settle on the problem at hand. To stop worrying about how they'd ever get another trap built instead of what to do right that second.

"How fast can you get that thing deployed, Rog? We may not be able to afford another chance at this."

He tapped his panel several times, face growing more pale by the second.

"Failsafe procedures push it out to about ten minutes. And raise the chance of success to near ninety-five percent."

"Without the failsafes?"

"Just under seven minutes should do it, if I can live with closer to fifty percent. I have to remind you black holes this small aren't supposed to be all that stable, Simmons. This space gullet has acted exactly the same in every other way. Radiation burst. Explosion."

"In theory, I know. I'm getting sick to death of that phrase."

Simmons took a deep breath. Her instincts were usually right when she trusted them. And she'd trusted Rog's brain way too often to stop now.

"Bring it in, Rog."

Simmons couldn't quite be gratified at seeing Rog's hands shake as he started work.

She wished she could hear the machinery in the back, even if it was nothing but the kind of humming and clicking that drove her nuts in a typical scouter. All she heard was Rog breathing. At least the smell of her own sweat drowned out his.

"Trap field established," he said.

Simmons zoomed in on the cylinder. The shape hadn't changed, but the whole thing had gone from transparent to milky and nearly opaque. She couldn't see any of the garbage through it at all.

With the *Treasure* alongside the creature now instead of head on, she could see the shape of the gap it created in space. It looked like a solid black funnel streaking away from the circular opening.

Even with the ship's lights on full power, the thing's mouth looked like nothing at all. It swallowed all the light and made Simmons's eyes ache. It was no wonder these things had been mistaken for black holes.

"Bring the trap forward, Simmons." Rog's voice trembled now. "Millisecond bursts, stop at thirty meters."

She tried to keep her eyes away from the trajectory of the tumbling waste box, visible in front of the *Treasure*. If they managed to pull this off, it would feed the creature and they'd be on their way. A meal that big might even help keep them safe for the next few days while they hauled their pet black hole away from here.

One hundred meters. Fifty.

"Hold," Rog said. "Let me try it from there."

Their opaque trap turned solid white now, like a perfect cylinder of ice in space. Rog tapped his panel a few times, then held his finger on a spot in the middle.

The trap and the creature stayed where they were. But a tinny alarm sounded from the panel.

"Still too far out," he said. "And that drained a lot of the power we're going to need. You have to bring it in closer, Simmons. Twenty-five meters. Best maneuvers of your life."

Simmons leaned down enough to block her own view out the window and the countdown clock, showing under two minutes. All she could focus on right now was the sensor display. She tapped the thruster, barely making contact.

Thirty-five meters.

Thirty.

Less than thirty seconds until impact.

The rogue garbage box had nearly reached the edge of the empty space in front of the creature. The eating zone. The box didn't curve toward the gravity pull. It continued on toward the trap.

"Be ready to turn it if this works," Rog said, leaning too close to Simmons's command chair. "We're out of time."

Simmons tapped the thruster one more time.

Twenty-seven meters would have to do.

"Now, Rog!"

A piercing wail broke through the highest level sound-proofing of any scouter in the solar system. The trap glowed red, then blue, shifting into purple.

The gap in space drifted backward toward the waiting trap, caught in a pull stronger than its own.

"If that noise stops and it turns black," Rog said, gripping her chair arm, "we have it. Be ready to turn it ninety degrees."

Simmons nodded, her finger hovering over the thruster. When the alarm abruptly cut out, the whole cylinder turned black. Before Rog could say a word, she rotated the trap.

The black hole creature devoured its final meal in deep space.

Chapter 5

Simmons missed the longer missions into space. She never missed having to take on the crap jobs no one else wanted because she was broke.

SimRog Disposal thrived even beyond what she or Rog expected. Planetary government contracts to clean up the garbage belt took them well past Jamison Wyatt's net worth in a couple of years. Corporate contracts to dispose of the most dangerous waste everywhere else took them beyond government wealth.

Those same governments agreed more readily than Simmons expected when she asked to keep her disposal technology private instead of sharing their designs with scientists. She answered their questions, sure. She even let them collect data from a distance.

But she wasn't about to let them think they had a chance to test just how unstable a micro black hole was. Nor was she going to admit what they actually had. Or pretend she could explain the difference between a black hole and their constantly hungry creature, currently anchored safely beyond Mars orbit.

Let them find their own wandering garbage disposal. Still…

Anything that eats has to excrete.

Simmons kept the obscure satellite report she'd run across to herself. What looked like a growing pond of sludge on Venus truly wasn't any of her concern, now was it?

It wasn't like people could land there anyway. No good reason to try on such a hellish place to begin with.

If their creature did eventually grow enough to shift where it dumped its steady diet of garbage, Simmons and Rog would both be long gone. If humans were as smart as they pretended to be, they'd have somewhere else to go besides Earth by then anyway. It had only grown a few millimeters in ten years' time.

She tried to never consider, not even in the privacy of her own mind, what might happen if the creature grew large enough to reproduce.

After all, humanity and all of life itself did leave garbage piles all over the place. From pre-history all the way into the distant, unknowable future.

Some things never changed.

SUNLIT
DISPOSITIONS
[A Hard-Boiled Space Opera]
JASON A. ADAMS

To the memory of Jim B.

Chapter 1

APRIL IS A FINE MONTH. On Vega 3 it's springtime, just like the northern parts of Old Earth. The planet was terraformed with standard Earth flora and fauna, so from the ground, you can't tell much difference. Tulips cover the ground in a red and yellow carpet, usually in the pattern of the Sunlit Spirits banner. Oak, alder, and ash trees spread their own yellow blanket over the land as their pollen engines go full throttle. The herbal smell of new plant growth tickles the nostrils, and honeysuckle fills with sweet nectar for children to suck. People walk barefoot through the parks, fresh grass tickling their toes. Chickadees, neo-robins, and a dozen other bird species fill the air with warbling songs. Vegan spring is gorgeous.

It was also fourteen light years away.

Me? I was stuck on a beat up cop boat full of a dozen beat up cops, no birds or flowers in sight. The most noticeable smell was the sweaty funk of twelve pairs of socks that needed washing. The birdsong consisted of an occasional announcement over the tinny squawkbox.

The things I do for a few hundred creds. I should've gone

into real estate.

My job was to figure out how an entire space station exploded. The Sunlit Station 23 turned the dark skies around the Capellan dwarf binary as bright as a nova four standard days ago. No warning, no communications from the station. Just an asteroid-sized fireball that lasted nearly five minutes.

The only thing the local authorities had to go on was a vid some bunch of wackos called the Oxfordians had sent to all the newscasters in the quadrant. A barely coherent screed about all the usual crap. Freedom of thought, freedom of movement. Free this and free that.

It's amazing what a person with the right amount of gumption will do.

Take this snafu, for example. A loose sphere about a hundred klicks wide. Spread through that whole area, chunks of charred metal, melted plastic, and forcibly separated human body parts.

Nasty stuff, but that's my job. My name's Alex, and I'm a Free Troubleshooter. What folks used to call a private investigator way back when. It keeps me out of trouble since I left the Spacer Marine Special Forces half a lifetime ago.

Ok, not free in the monetary sense. Free in that I'm not beholden to the Sunlit Spirits empire, outside of contractual obligation when I'm on a job for them.

I was on the Sunlit Ship *Acceptance*, a fast cutter assigned for my use by the Capellan Keepers of the Way, the local cops. They were fine for the usual petty nonsense, like stolen ink pens or candy bars, but no way could they handle a blown up space station.

That's why the regional Higher Power called me. Well, to be precise, the HP's lackey called me. The farther up the food chain people get, the less work they want to do.

If I'd known what I was in for, I wouldn't have taken the job.

Chapter 2

THE CALL CAME three days ago, at just the right time. I'd been sitting in my squeaky wooden chair at my battered plaswood desk. Good thing the plaswood was mahogany colored all the way through. A kitten could get lost in some of the dents and scratches.

I say my desk and chair because those were the only things left in the office that I owned. My spot was in a rundown building at the intersection of Winos and Hookers in downtown New Clintwood, Vega 3's capitol.

For a planet run by iron-fisted abolitionists, Vega 3 has plenty of both.

I was wondering how I'd pay the rent this month. Worse, I was down to my last bottle of hypergin, and the fridge was empty. That's when my secretary buzzed through in my cochlear comlink.

"Call for you, Alex," she said in that husky contralto voice that sends shivers down my spine.

"Thanks, Kandi," I said. "Wanna fool around later?"

"Sorry, Boss," she replied, like she always does. "I've got a hot date with your hovercar."

I should point out that for all her sexy voice, Kandi is my electronic assistant. Her body doesn't match her voice at all, given that she's in a ten centimeter black quartzene case I carry in my pocket. Pity.

If I got a little ahead on expenses, I could save up for an android body for her, and—

"Alex here," I said shaking my head as I flicked my ear, activating the external com. I never use vid, only voice. "What can I do ya for?"

I have a last name, but here in SS territory, surnames are outlawed. Kind of a weird tradition, but there are a lot more of them than of me, so I play along.

"Alex, this is Gene, Galactic Service Representative for SS District 17," said a booming baritone, rich and full and from the gut. The voice of someone who often speaks before large crowds of mindless followers. A GSR instead of an Assembly rep, though. Higher Power, not a Highest Power. Middle management.

"Greetings, Gene," I said, trying to keep the annoyance out of my tone. "Have you wronged me and need to make amends?"

"Do not be flippant with me," Gene said, voice dropping a few frosty degrees. "I no longer have any amends to make."

Translation: *I don't apologize to people. People apologize to me.* I can't believe anyone falls for these idiots.

"We need you to investigate a problem out in the Capella B system," Gene said. "We would like you to leave at once. Time may be of the essence."

"Cap B?" I asked. "There's nothing out there but a refit and refuel station, is there?"

"There was, yes." The old fraud cleared his throat, hesitated, and went on.

"Day before yesterday, with no warning at all, the station

exploded. We need you to find those responsible and bring them to us."

"What part of the station blew?" I asked. "Was it the reactor? Crew quarters? What?"

"The station exploded, Alex. The whole station. Kaboom. Nothing left bigger than five meters wide or so."

Yeah, that was bad all right.

"Any leads?" I asked.

"Only one," Gene replied. "A vid was sent to all the news outlets. I'll beam it to you. Check it out on your way over, see what you think."

Nice try, Gene.

"First, we need to discuss my fee," I said. "Anyone who could do something like this is a danger to my tender and delicate bod. Five hundred credits a day, plus expenses."

From the choked splutters, I figured Gene might be having a heart attack.

"*Five?*" he finally shouted. "Last time you only charged two!"

"Last time, I only had to bring home a couple of errant alcolytes who snuck off on an Altairan freighter and found the crew's suprabourbon," I reminded him. "This time it's five hundred, per standard twenty-four hour daycycle, mind, and you can pay three days up front. That'll cover my time there and back. I'll bill the rest at weekly intervals."

Gene grumbled and groused for a while, but only to save face. We both knew I was the only FT in Sigma Quandrant willing to work for the Sunlit Spirits. Only reason I would is because after growing up with a crackpot granddad who went to every subversive fundamentalist revival in half the galaxy, the Sunlits were pretty easy for me to ignore. Their proselytizing was more of the slow and steady type, rather than a smack in the face with hellfire and brimstone. They were all cut from the same sackcloth, though.

No matter how advanced we get, there are always superstitious wingnuts and plenty of book-waving grifters ready to fleece the sheep.

After a few more minutes of calm determination from me and uncalm apoplexy from Gene, we had a deal. I waited until Kandi told me the first payment was in the account. Only took ten minutes. Ol' Gene must really be desperate.

I went upstairs to my apartment and grabbed a few spare duds and my favorite charcoal-gray neocotton sport jacket, the one with the cream-colored Mekbuda ivory buttons and the oversized inner lapel pocket on the left side.

I also grabbed my peacemaker, a custom-made Smith-Westfall Spaceway Patrol model. Twenty-five 5mm frangible slugs per magazine, plus an underslung double-barrel gamma pulse beamer. It just so happens the gun fits perfectly in that big lapel pocket I mentioned.

Confidence. Don't leave home without it.

"I have the shuttle information, Alex," Kandi said in my ear. "Docking bay ninety-four. Shall I call an autocab?"

"What about my hovercar?"

"Sorry, boss. I wore the poor thing out." Kandi said. She never laughed or giggled, but I think she would if she could. My hovercar hadn't hovered in several months. This job might pay enough to fix the old heap.

The autocab showed up five minutes later, and I was off.

Chapter 3

THE TRIP to Capella A1 where I was to meet Gene only took seventeen hours, give or take. Most of that was getting to the shuttle bay and riding the shuttle to the nearest peoplenexus. Fortunately, I can sleep on demand, so the transit part went by pretty quickly.

I did remember to watch the vid Gene had sent me. I had Kandi pipe it to my berth's screen. A masked face appeared, probably male given the size and squareness of the head. The black knit toboggan pulled over his face was a nicely retro touch, but also practical. Any digital distortion could be undone by a good video processor. A physical disguise was impenetrable.

As far as the message, it was typical manifesto-type drivel. The figure droned on and on about how the Sunlit Spirits had twisted the original message of a group called the Oxfordians and needed to be punished. How all would be forgiven if control of all SS worlds was handed over to the Oxfordians. How the Oxfordians didn't want any more bloodshed, but were perfectly happy to blow more stuff up if the Sunlits didn't step into line.

I'm paraphrasing, but that was the general gist. I went through the whole thing a couple more times, then took a nap. I didn't bother waking up until Kandi buzzed me to let me know we'd arrived.

The nexus is nothing more than a plain waiting room a couple of AUs from Vega 3. A mini-space station. The Vegan nexus is like most of the others. A hundred-meter-long tube of double-hulled plasteel. Fluorescent yellow reflective coating makes it easy to spot from a distance.

Inside, it's mainly one big hall with the same cheap metal and fabric chairs that have been numbing people's butts in municipal structures for half a millennium. Travel ads showing happy families in a dizzying array of climates and topographies cover the industrial green walls. There's a planet for everyone, and the nexus can get you there.

I had priority, which earned me a few dozen withering glares from the others waiting their turns. I stepped to the actual nexus, a small cubby about the size of an average elevator, scanned my palm and went inside.

A brief feeling of being turned inside out and rolled up like a windowshade, and I was at the Capellan nexus. Sounds worse than it feels. You get used to it.

I left the cubicle, popping a couple of anti-nausea tabs as I entered a waiting room exactly like the one I'd left. Different people in the chairs, different posters on the walls. Plus, a man-high banner proclaiming "WELCOME TO THE CAPELLA SYSTEM. PLEASE DON'T FORGET TO DISCARD ANY FRUITS OR VEGETABLES BEFORE DEPARTING THE NEXUS."

I have to keep Kandi turned off when I'm around SS muckity-mucks. They aren't big on most labor-saving tech. Something about doing things the hard way being good for the soul or some such nonsense. Turns out I didn't need her this time, though.

A man in a well-tailored double-breasted suit in royal blue waited for me. The suit—not to mention the three guys in Initiate yellow hovering nearby—worked better than if he'd held a placard with my name on it.

"You must be Gene," I said, striding toward him with my hand outstretched. "Alex, licensed Free Troubleshooter."

Gene grabbed my hand in a strong grip, pumped it twice, exactly three inches up and three down.

"Glad you're here, Alex," he said. "We've got a ship from the Capellan Keepers of the Way. It's all yours as long as you need it. You can head straight to what's left of Station 23."

Chapter 4

So that's why I was here aboard the *Acceptance*, staring at a cloud of metallic and fleshy debris. I needed to get to work. The cloud was already starting to swirl into Capella B's gravity well. At least cleanup wouldn't be a problem.

I had Tony, the ship's sensor genius, analyze the immediate area. The only things unexpected this close to a brown dwarf were high levels of oxidized tetrahexamine, an extraordinarily flammable compound normally used in Hi-Thrust fuel for unmanned cargo transports, and noticeable amounts of carbon dioxide and nitrogen oxides. Common gases, but not so common in these levels out in space.

I asked Captain Thomas, a short but stocky man with the weathered toughness of an old oak stump, to have his folks check through local chemical supply and transfer logs. He wore the deeper blue of a higher level Higher Power, so I figured he had pretty good connections.

"No problem," he said. "What are we looking for?"

"People without intra-system rockets buying rocket fuel," I said. "Not to mention shipments of chloritol, nitric acid, anything you don't normally find at your local grocer."

I was a few years away from combat engineer training, but this had all the signs of sabotage.

Ok, so the vid from the Oxfordians was another hint. Sue me for wanting to feel clever sometimes.

Tony ran a full spectrographic analysis on the debris field before the Sunlit tugships starting pushing the mess into the nearby star. He didn't find anything else I wouldn't expect to see, but better safe than sorry.

"Where is the closest Oxfordian cell?" I asked Thomas. His search hadn't turned up any odd shipments in the Capella system, so the stuff had come in from outside.

"Antares 7," the captain replied with no hesitation. "Led by a man named Peter, who is a Johnson, and his wife Jolene."

"Peter Johnson," I said. "People outside the Sunlit Empire use both given and surname, you know."

Thomas shuddered. I've never understood the taboo against surnames, but it runs deep in these folks.

"Can you change the markings and digital signatures on the *Acceptance?*" I asked. "Or get me a non-descript civilian sedan-jumper? I doubt a planet that shelters the Oxfordians would welcome a Sunlit cutter."

"We can keep it simple, Alex," Thomas said, clapping me on the shoulder. "We can convert this ship to an Antarean family boat in no time." He muttered some orders to a lieutenant with an initiate's yellow acorns on his lapels, who saluted and started yelling at the brown-clad alcolyte crew.

I watched as Wilson, the comms officer, rattled keys and altered the *Acceptance's* call and beacon signals. Outside, two men in self-propelled EVA suits slapped new decals over the Sunlit markings. They also changed the numbers on the prow.

In less than thirty minutes, the *Acceptance* had become

the *Barfly*, a sport-utility recreational vehicle registered out of Antares Prime.

"That's pretty impressive," I told Captain Thomas. I meant it, too. "But I thought the Sunlit Spirit empire prides itself on rigorous honesty."

"Of course we do," Thomas said with a serene smile. "I'm not going to come out and *say* we're not an SS ship. I simply know the Antarean border patrols aren't going to ask. They don't think we'd repaint our hull either."

"You sure about this?" I asked.

"Trust me," he said. "We do this all the time."

Which is a statement designed to make any sane person nervous.

Chapter 5

THE TRIP to the Antares system only took twelve standard hours, since the local vessel-nexus was less than a megaklick away. Thomas' people at Sunlit Intelligence had nothing concrete on unusual shipments, which wasn't surprising since I figured it wasn't an in-system job.

I sat at a spare gunner's mate station and tried not to be bored to death on a ship full of teetotalling religious zealots. I could hear them chanting the whole time. Steps, traditions, prayers… Fortunately, I still had a flask of hypergin, a pocket full of breath mints, and quick hands.

And I wasn't bored for long.

As soon as we passed through the nexus, a sleek corvette stood off and fired a particle beam across our bow.

A chime split the stunned silence. Incoming hail. Thomas flicked a hand at Wilson, who opened the channel and threw it to screen. A young soldier with perfectly edged red hair and a green uniform that matched his eyes shimmered into view. He had silver eagles on his epaulets. Antarean sub-Commandant. Pretty big bug to be driving a border 'vette.

"-is SC Wilhelm Strauss, commanding the AS *Sentinel.*

Leave your engines idle and prepare to be boarded. Repeat. This is SC Wilhelm Strauss, commanding the AS—"

"Darn it!" Thomas said under his breath, then louder. "This is Thomas H. Power. What reason do you have to board us?"

"Simple," Strauss said. "This is the fourth time this year the *Barfly* has entered our space. This is only the second time the name has matched your ship's particular outline. That, and the unfortunate incident with SS 23 a few days ago makes me wonder if you might not actually be Sunlighters snooping around. Are you in fact Sunlit Spirits?"

Thomas' face contorted like he'd just bitten into a lemon. I could see him trying not to tell the truth.

"I…that is, we…dang it! I refuse to answer your question." Thomas was red and sweating with effort. How the hell had the SS empire survived for nearly two hundred years?

"You just did," Strauss said. "Not to mention, voice print analysis shows you as Higher Power Thomas, Captain of the SS *Acceptance* of the 18th Capellan Keepers of the Way. And *that* makes you a violator of the SS-Antares peace treaty, section 8, subparagraph C, which states that no officer or vessel of the SS military or government may enter Antares space without proper authorization."

"You and your crew are under arrest, Captain Thomas."

Chapter 6

"Now WHAT?" I asked. I patted the pistol in my pocket. Still there, still loaded.

"There is no 'now what'," Thomas said in a resigned tone. "We broke the rules, we have to face the consequences. Probably a fine and public humiliation for the Council. Loss of rank and command for me. Or maybe a firing squad from our new friends on the *Sentinel.*"

"Like hell," I snapped. "This heap has guns, right? Missiles, maybe? Let's blast our way back through the nexus and—"

"No can do," Thomas said, raising a hand to silence me. "We need to promptly admit our wrongs and make restitution."

"Up yours, wacko," I said. I ran to the nav console, knocked some poor sap whose name I didn't recall out of the chair, and punched the code for all ahead full.

The cutter shot forward like a cheetah that backed into a hot poker.

Straight at the 'vette.

Oops.

They must have figured we'd try something. A hail of particle beam fire tore through the *Acceptance* before we closed half the distance.

Dull explosions ripped through the hull, from the stern.

From the engines.

We were suddenly dead in space, our forward drift slowed by a reverse tractor beam from the Antarean ship.

Thomas glared at me. The other Sunlits looked at us and at each other, lost for ideas.

I pulled my gun and ran from the bridge, looking for a place to hole up until the excitement was over.

I ducked into a low supply bin near the main airlock just as a docking collar clanged into place on the other side. The bin contained nothing but a bunch of mildewy pamphlets, all pimping some bit of SS dogma or another. I flipped through a few while booted feet tromped back and forth between the airlock and bridge.

I wondered if the pamphlets had been written for mental defectives. Bunch of cultspeak hooey.

Once things were silent for a good five minutes, I finally came out. I crouched low, pistol in hand, and went for the airlock and docking collar. Both ships' locks were still connected and open, so we hadn't started moving yet.

I crept through, my gaze flicking around like a drunk moth in a candle factory.

No one here, no noise.

Up a level, moving toward the bridge.

Silence.

No, not silence.

A few meters ahead, I could hear voices coming from a room to the left. One loud and angry, one calm and almost bored.

"The Oxfordians, probably at Johnson's orders, destroyed SS 23 and killed everyone on board!" That was Thomas. No mistaking that tone of no-longer-in-control-but-still-self-righteous.

"The Oxfordians haven't existed for over two hundred years." Strauss.

"You're a liar!" Thomas shouted. "Admit it! Your kind don't know how to be honest."

"Have you bothered to ask yourself why anyone would bother attacking the Sunlits?" Strauss said. He sounded sincerely curious. "I mean, you don't have wealth, you don't control huge swathes of territory, no remarkable mineral deposits. Just a handful of fairly plain, ordinary worlds."

"We have plenty," Thomas said, a little huffy and defensive now. "Our people are honest and hard working. Our worlds are peaceful and chock full of good farmland. Our—"

"Yes, yes, that's all true. So why would anyone want to blow up a space station of yours? Maybe your Free Troubleshooter out there in the corridor has an answer."

Shit. It figured. Probably cameras all up and down this tub.

I uncrouched myself and joined the two officers. I still had my peacemaker in hand, though. Thomas's eyes widened when he saw it. Struass spared it a glance, but that was about it.

"So tell me, O Investigator," Strauss said to me. "Can you think of any good reason?"

Both he and Thomas looked straight at me. I ran over it, looking at it from all the angles. Only one thing really made any sense.

"I can, actually," I said. Strauss raised his left eyebrow. Neat trick.

Thomas looked relieved, at least until I finished.

"The Sunlits themselves blew it up," I said. "Sent a fake terrorist vid to the news outlets first, so everyone would know the Oxfordians are back."

"What do you mean, back?" Thomas said, spluttering over the words as his face went a tad blotchy. "The Oxfordians were never gone! They have always sought to overthrow the Empire. Ever since The Founder received his vision of the Truth and left their group, taking most of their followers—"

"Have you ever read any history books not approved by the Empire's General Service Committee?" I asked. "I'd never heard of the Oxfordians until Gene sent me that vid. Empire texts are full of references to them, though. Quite a boogeyman for you folks."

"I…you…all Truth comes directly from The Founder!" Thomas finally managed. "Only His Way, as laid down in The Book and transmitted down through the Higher Powers is real. All else is false. Cunning traps laid by the powerful to baffle the Faithful."

"Yeah, right," I said. "Doesn't the planet Joyous in the Capella B system manufacture a metric shit ton of tetra-hexamine?"

"Well, yes, I suppose it does," Thomas said, looking nervous.

"And the planet Free manufactures chlorate, which requires quite a bit of nitric acid to process," Strauss added. "We did our own scans of the debris field."

Thomas jumped to his feet. "You violated the treaty first, you jerk!"

"No we didn't," Strauss said, still half bored. "We used civilian scientific research ships. No military or government personnel anywhere on board."

"Anyway," Thomas said, changing the subject. "Why would the Sunlit Spirits blow up our own station? Unless it was an accident they didn't want to admit to, although that wouldn't be very honest."

"I hate to break it to you, Thomas," Strauss said, not unkindly. "Most of the people at the District Leadership level and higher are politicians first, Sunlit Spirits second. They could very easily have destroyed the station simply to plant the fear of further Oxfordian attacks in the minds of your people. Fear of a common enemy has always been the best way to keep a populace in line. Keep them from asking questions."

"Asking questions is a sign of overthinking," Thomas said automatically, like a coin-op fortune cookie machine. "It's better to just do what you're told and pray for guidance, instead of complicating things."

Thomas suddenly grabbed for my right hand. My shooting hand.

I pulled the secondary trigger. Two violet gamma pulse bursts hit him right below his triangular Sunlit Spirits medallion, throwing him backward.

He hit the ground, arms and legs flopping.

"I don't think we can do anything for him," I said to Strauss. "Sounds like he's too far gone." I checked him out, made sure the gammas hadn't done more than knock him out.

"We'll send him and his crew back home," Strauss said. "We'll impound the ship, of course."

"And me?" I asked.

"We intercept enough SS transmissions to know you were only hired for window dressing," he said. "You're free to leave. Pity you can't keep the 'investigation' going. You might have milked the Empire for scads of credits."

"Or I might have been another unfortunate victim of the evil Oxfordians," I said. I couldn't help but smile.

"Mind dropping me off at the nearest peoplenexus?"

Chapter 7

So that was that. I got back to Vega 3 fifteen hundred credits richer, but without the likelihood of any more contracts from the Sunlits. That was fine with me. I spent the evening downing most of a bottle of Galax Hypergin '45, nice and fresh, less than a month from the distillery.

Nothing about the station or the incident with the *Acceptance* made the news. I wasn't surprised. The Antareans didn't care, and the Sunlits weren't about to admit anything. I wouldn't say anything, either. Not good business to bandy client secrets about.

I turned Kandi back on. Well, I turned the box in my pocket back on. Kandi lives out in the ethercloud somewhere.

"How we doing, doll?" I said, only hiccupping once. "In the black for a change?"

"Yes, Alex," she said. "In fact, after paying the rent for the next quarter and arranging repairs on your hovercar, you have a profit of sixty-seven credits."

Good thing hypergin doesn't stain, because I sprayed about half the room.

"*How* much? How the hell did rent and a new actuator drain me that badly?" I finished off the bottle. "Goddamn ripoff artists! every one of 'em oughtta be—"

"Well," Kandi purred. "I might have found a great deal on an android body for a certain indispensible assistant. One with long legs and programmable hair, skin tone, and measurements."

I sat down again. Okay, maybe I fell a little bit. Missed the chair. Good shit, that hypergin.

"Kandi, my dear," I said. "I can't wait to finally meet you."

ABOUT KARI

A science fiction fan from the first time she caught a grainy black and white rerun of *Lost in Space*, Kari Kilgore's wanderlust and imagination lead her all over the world on grand adventures. Her heart and family bring her home to her native Appalachian Mountains of Virginia. From that solid base, she and her husband Jason A. Adams bring those adventures to life in fiction.

Kari writes science fiction, fantasy, romance, and contemporary fiction, and she's happiest when she surprises herself. She lives at the end of a long dirt road in the middle of the woods with Jason, various house critters, and wildlife they're better off not knowing more about.

The Confidential Adventure Club

For Kari's exclusive free After The End stories and deleted scenes, discounts, early pre-sale releases, adorable pet photos, and a whole lot more not available anywhere else, pay a visit to The Confidential Adventure Club at www.smarturl.it/c-a-club.

Hope to see you there!

www.karikilgore.com
www.spiralpublishing.net

ABOUT JASON

Jason A. Adams grew up a military brat, a life that exposed him to many places, people from around the world, and a lifetime curiosity that informs his fiction.

Jason's writing includes one novella and many short stories based in and around the Virginia coalfields he lives in and loves. He currently lives on a forest mountain with his beautiful wife, Kari Kilgore, also a writer of many wonderful stories.

You can keep up with Jason's news, upcoming fiction, travel adventures, and whatever else strikes his fancy at www.BrainSquirrelBriefings.com.

To see more of Jason's and Kari's fiction, go to
www.SpiralPublishing.net
news@jasonadams.info

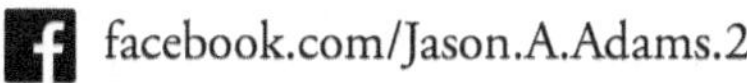 facebook.com/Jason.A.Adams.2

ALSO BY KARI KILGORE

I hope you enjoyed *Near Future Forward* as much as I enjoyed writing it. For more space opera and galactic empire stories, be sure to keep an eye out for Dispatches from the Galaxy at www.dispatchesfromthegalaxy.com.

For more science fiction from both me and Jason A. Adams, visit Spiral Publishing's Science Fiction page at www.spiralpublishing.net/book-tag/science-fiction.

Be the first to know about release dates and check out more of my fiction across almost every genre at www.karikilgore.com.

The Confidential Adventure Club

Want more fiction from Kari, including stories, discounts, and box sets not available anywhere else? Want to hear about locations, research, and other cool things that inspired this story and beyond? Want all that and adorable pet photos, too?

Join The Confidential Adventure Club and get a thank you gift of a free short story and a whole lot more at www.smarturl.it/c-a-club.

Hope to see you there!

Dispatches from the Galaxy Stories:

Restricted Species

The Becalmed

The Garbage Belt

Plurapod Pathogen

The Changes Cascade

The Storms of Future Past Series:

Dreaming the Storm

Joining the Storm

Into the Storm

Fighting the Storm

Sensing the Storm: A Storms of Future Past Prequel Story

Storms of the Heart: A Storms of Future Past Romance

Storms of Future Past Books One through Four Collection

The Voices through Time Series:

Songs in the Mountain

Secrets in the Land

Walking the Ghosts: A Voices through Time Novella

Terminalia Short Stories:

Terminalia

Little Five

Novels:

Until Death

The Dream Thief

Hand Me Downs

Novellas:

Legacy of the Land

In the Pines

DNA Never Lies

Collections:

Fantastic Women: A Dark Fantasy Novella Trio

Fantastic Shorts: Volume 1

Near Future Forward (with Jason A. Adams)

Fantastic Shorts: Volume 2

Partners in Romance (with Jason A. Adams)

Short Stories:

Renovations, Intentions, The Seeds of Love, Wicked Bone, The Sound of Murder, Reflections, The Last Dragonkeeper, The Earworms, Odds and Endings, Dawn Visitor, The Spider Who Ate the Elephant, The Worry Trap, An Adventure Well Begun, Morning Glory, The Heart Is the Strongest, The Sweetest Trouble, Happily Ever After in KrampusLand, The Real Treasure in Cairo, Soul Deep

ALSO BY JASON A. ADAMS

I hope you enjoyed reading the stories in *Near Future Forward* as much as I enjoyed writing them.

Visit www.jasonadams.info and join the adventure for exclusive new fiction, my past and future travels, and whatever else strikes my fancy. Hope to see you there!

Novellas:

Agonist

Short Stories:

Mick of Malvern: Seeker for Hire (A Hard-Boiled Fairy Tale)

To Catch a Thief (An Appalachian Gothic Tale)

Sunlit Dispositions (A Hard-Boiled Space Opera)

GS-304

Angel of Mercy

ADDITIONAL COPYRIGHT INFORMATION